ENDORSEMENTS

"Cappas hit a home run! Reads like a modern *Screwtape Letters*."

—BRENT SLADE, FCA Urban Baseball Director Atlanta,
UGA Alum

"Cappas awakens our imagination to the reality of spiritual warfare. *Heaven Breaks In* reminds us that our battle is not against flesh and blood, and he who is in us is greater than the one who is in the world."

—ROBBY HIGGINBOTTOM, College Minister,
Park Cities Presbyterian Church, PCA Dallas TX, Duke Alum

"Inspired by the literary genius of CS Lewis, Cappas skillfully takes the *Screwtape Letters* and turns it on its head. Captivating to the heart and mind, *Heaven Breaks In* masterfully affirms God's wisdom and presence victorious over life's challenges."

—JANA HARMON, Teaching Fellow, CS Lewis Institute of Atlanta,
PhD Apologetics Candidate, University of Birmingham, England

"Cappas weaves the truth of Scripture beautifully into the life and story of his protagonist Davis. A powerful aid to help us see our world through a biblical lens."

—CAROLINE WHITE, RUF Campus Ministry,
Mississippi State University, SMU Alum

"Intriguing story, fascinating characters. This book's bound for Hollywood."

—CHRIS MILHOUS, Former CEO of Ogilvy & Mather Atlanta,
Managing Principal of MB Global House, Bucknell Alum

"A powerful story showing the biblical truth that God fights on our behalf. And a clever look at how spiritual warfare is tied to our human weakness and the world's deceptive philosophies. A must read for any high school or college student!

—CLAY FUQUA, Director of Bridges Student Ministry, Georgia Tech, UAB Alum

"A masterfully orchestrated depiction of the struggle, salvation, and redemption of the Christian in the modern world. *Heaven Breaks In* is both a challenge and an encouragement to anyone who has ever wrestled with the purpose of his own existence."

—WILSON WAGGONER, University of Virginia Alum, Former President of Kappa Sigma Fraternity, Citibank Energy Analyst

"A stirring reminder of the warfare we face. Cappas has the piercing insight of a first-rate scriptwriter. Christian storytelling just reached new heights!"

—ANNA JULISE COOK, Professional Actor, Lee University Alum

"*Heaven Breaks In* pulls the curtain back on the reality of life as a college freshman. As the story unfolds you will be drawn in, find the book hard to put down, and discover spiritual insights that might just change the way you view and live life."

—JASON ELLERBEE, Young Couples Pastor, Briarwood Presbyterian Church, PCA, Birmingham Alabama, UGA Alum

Heaven Breaks In

A Novel

NICHOLAS CAPPAS

To C.S. Lewis,

Who wrote for the Glory of God

and paved the way for many of us.

ACKNOWLEDGMENTS

I would like to thank Jesus Christ, my Lord and Savior; my exceptional editor, K. B. Hoyle, who worked tirelessly and wrote the initial drafts of Davis's journal entries; Anne Corbitt, who weighed in on style and voice; Jessica Coleman, for enhancing plot structure; the Core Collective writing group in Atlanta for reviewing letter drafts and spurring me on; Kevin Marks for his publishing wisdom and guidance; Robert E. Lee's writings on strategy and warfare; *Chariots of Fire* for inspiration; the Universities and Churches that have nurtured my growth; and all of my friends and family who have offered guidance, prayer, and encouragement along the way, especially my parents.

* Writer's Note: Though spiritual warfare is real on college campuses, this book is entirely fictional.

Remember Creation

When the God of Angel Armies formed us,
and by His Holiness allowed us to witness His Divine Artistry:

When He laid the foundation of the earth,
when He determined its measurements,
and stretched the line upon it.

When He drew a circle on the face of the deep,
when He made firm the skies above,
when He established the fountains of the deep,
when He assigned to the sea its limit,
so that the waters might not transgress His command,
when He marked out the foundation of the earth.

And then, when He made a human,
from the dust of the earth,
and breathed life into him.

We rejoiced in His inhabited world
and delighted in the children of man.

And we cheered for them.

And remember last night when our multitudes sang praises in the celestial choir,

"Glory to God. Glory to God, in the Highest, and Peace, on Earth. Good Will toward Men."

We sang in perfect harmony; our crescendo shook the Heavens; pure, bright light flashed across the Sky.

The humans, they know not such perfection. The sons of men, they live without a love free from conditions. The children of God, they sojourn in an imperfect world, tainted by sin. At times, it scares them.

Holy Angel, Chosen Messenger by our Lord,

You are leaving our heavenly world and all of its beauty, splendor, and perfection

to fly down and to minister alongside those we have loved from the beginning.

You will bring the Peace and Goodwill of which we sing to one Special human being.

Littleton, I have been summoned to serve as your mentor on your first angelic assignment. Please know I'm overseeing several worldwide campaigns aimed at attacking spiritually dark spheres of society wherein the Gospel has little penetration. In each of these campaigns I will be mentoring selected angels; our correspondence will be shared with every angel throughout the campaign. To change the character of the war we need to push back evil and gain significant ground that's been lost. In some of these situations–as with sex trafficking–the sin is gross and obvious, and we simply do not have enough human intervention. In other arenas, sin can be cleverly masked and society may be unable to see the darkness that hides behind happy facades. But warfare exists just the same. Such is the case with many college students on university campuses today. This brings us to Davis and to your university assignment.

Young Davis, though learned in the Holy Scripture, does not fathom the battles occurring in the spiritual realms. Occasionally he hears a sermon preached. He may catch a glimpse here or there from Bible readings, but he has no idea of the war raging around him. The angels and demons fighting in his midst. Horses and chariots battling in the heavens.

So, today I released several Angelic Warriors in the celestial realm to clash with fallen angels over this assignment. You should have seen how eager they were to join in the fight. I handpicked this team, choosing a seasoned legion accustomed to being outnumbered; they set the sky ablaze when they took off.

Littleton, you'll be on the ground. You're stationed on campus with Davis. A lot of your battle will be in the mind. Satan's typical strategy in this culture is to have his demons hit subjects such as Davis daily, with temptations, distractions, and discouraging messages, trying to lead them astray. So you will have to know Davis well enough for your counter-messages to be effective.

Lift him up and keep him mindful of God. We need your eye for detail and your cleverness, your ability to read Davis better than the demons do, to deliver messages two to three steps ahead of them. Davis won't be able to see you; in fact, he won't even know you exist. And since you don't have the ability to read his mind, you'll need to observe him closely. Watch his facial expressions, notice his vocal inflections, and trace his footsteps to see where he walks.

As you engage in the spirit wars, send me brief summary reports of Davis's activities. When doing so, think of me as a senior strategist and lean on me for insight. Ask whatever questions cross your mind. I can guide your thought patterns and direct your focus. And I will speak and write to you in common, earthly language so you learn to live, think and breathe as one closest to their ranks.

Most respectfully your humble servant,
Archangel Michael

August 25

Littleton,

As you settle in, meditate on this section of Davis's spiritual biography:

Davis Lewis Chandler was born in Atlanta, Georgia, and grew up in a white Georgian-style home that his parents purchased before he was born. His father, Elliot, and his mother, Marianne, have a good marriage but live a hurried life, causing them to fall short of the unsearchable riches of resting in the love of Christ alone.

Throughout Davis's childhood his family attended a church comprised primarily of the historic families of the area. Most church members have abundant wealth and are highly conscious of how society works, and they rarely rely on our Lord for guidance. Deep, personal religion is primarily for the clergy, and the typical member thinks Jesus only expects them to be good, moral citizens. Sunday is the Lord's Day, but He does not get called upon too often Monday through Saturday. I'm sure you can imagine the spiritual void the practices of this church leaves in the soul of its members.

Davis is the oldest of two and is quite close to his younger sister, Ansley. He was an extremely intelligent, friendly, well-rounded teenager. October of his sophomore year in high school, however, is the key to understanding his development. Returning home after a lacrosse match (and driving separately from the team), one of Davis's teammates was hit in a head-on collision and died on impact. The accident unsettled Davis. Of course, he grieved for his friend. But every time a community member mentioned the death, Davis would say to himself, "That could have been me." The thought gnawed at him. Perhaps for the first time in his life, Davis realized his mortality.

At the funeral service, the youth minister–an insightful young man named Jason Allison–preached a message discussing how human vulnerability and brokenness expose a person's deep need and natural longing for the love of God. "Times of brokenness expose the deep hole we all feel in our hearts, a God-shaped hole that can only be filled by Christ alone," he spoke with confidence.

Davis felt as though Jason was preaching directly to him. After the service he immediately walked through the crowd and introduced himself, shaking the minister's hand. Sensing this was an emotional time for Davis, Jason invited him to lunch. This meal began a friendship that changed the course of Davis's teenage years and put him a few steps spiritually removed from many of his friends, and even his family. Along with his passion for lacrosse, Davis began attending youth retreats, Bible studies, and mission trips. He also formed a close, authentic friendship with another student from the minister's youth group, named Jonathan Clarkston.

By his senior year, Davis wrote in a letter to his parents during a weekend retreat, "I have learned to sing 'Amazing grace, how sweet the sound that saved a wretch like me' and to know what it means."

Our Lord has big plans for Davis. Please know that he has the spiritual gift of leadership and has that rare quality of being able to move within influential circles, yet stand independently from his peers. You are to help Davis grow closer to Jesus and to nurture his leadership gifts during this formative time. Satan and his host of fallen angels, of course, will battle at all costs to distract him from his calling.

Davis hopes to join a college ministry that will continue the spiritual legacy of his youth group. He already has one group targeted. Two previous graduates from his high school are active in what's called "The Edge," the largest student ministry on campus. They invited him to attend the group's first meeting for the semester.

Littleton, your time has arrived. Our angelic team is on campus awaiting your presence. Watch and observe. Ask questions. Dig deep into the culture you are assigned and focus on your man. Send me a summary letter of Davis's week.

Archangel Michael (hereafter *AM*)

August 29

Archangel Michael,

Lots to tell.

On Saturday morning, Davis and his family carried his clothes, a tennis racquet and lacrosse stick, his Bible, and a few other books through the hallway of Clifton Dorm and into room #206. By the smile on his face and the pace at which he moved his belongings from the U-haul into the room, I'd say Davis's enthusiasm for his new environment was quite obvious.

Departures were bittersweet. As they unloaded the last few boxes and walked back to the car, his father said, "That should do it, son. Looking forward to hearing from you soon."

A few moments of silence followed, then Davis filled the gap by saying, "Thanks. Thanks for everything. I really love y'all. We'll talk. A lot." He hugged each of them.

"Oh Davis, you'll do great here!" his mother said with tears in her eyes.

The longest of Davis's three hugs went to his younger sister, which he followed by saying, "Ansley, I can't wait to hear from you. You're going to love this year. Jesus will guide your steps."

His family departed to let Davis take care of his room.

When I look at Davis I see a young man on a mission. He rises fairly early and spends the day trying to reduce his checklist and build new friendships. And I just love him. You should've seen Davis on Tuesday at the student events fair, approaching tables, talking and laughing, asking questions and sharing stories. The look on his face seemed to say, "I can't wait to find my place here." His enthusiasm and youthful innocence disarms people.

Walking home from the fair, Davis's best friend Jonathan called. "Davis, how've you been, bro?"

"Jonathan! Awesome! It's going to be a great year. Guess what? My roommate Andrew's a Christian. We've been going to The Edge together. And I just signed up to rush several of the fraternities I met with this summer."

"That's great. I know Christ is going to use you in that place! I can't wait to hear about it. Hey, there's another reason I'm calling. I've been asked to help organize a mission trip to an orphanage in Kenya for spring break. I'd love for you to come with us. Jason is going, along with Amanda, Will, Anne and several others from our youth group. I thought you might like to be a part of the team. Pray about it."

"Of course!" Davis said. "I don't even need to pray about it. I've always wanted to go to Africa. Serving in Kenya sounds amazing."

"Awesome! I'll set up an online link to share so we can raise our support as a team. I'll be sending out information soon–forms to fill out, medical vaccinations needed, and short spiritual devotionals for us to read every month."

"Not a problem. I'm already pumped!"

"All right!" Jonathan laughed. "Well, that was easy. I'll talk to you again soon, brother."

"Yep. Talk to you later."

Archangel Michael, I couldn't be happier that Davis is going on this mission trip over his first college spring break. And that he's staying connected with Jonathan, who is studying for ministry at a Christian university and is in a more nurturing environment than he is.

It hasn't all been smooth sailing, though. With the comforts of home and his youth community severed, enemy forces–and there are many of them here–seized the opportunity and exploited the void left behind. They incited a rivalry between Davis and his roommate, Andrew Mason. Andrew grows jealous when other students enjoy Davis's company and give him attention. Like yesterday, for example, when a young lady from The Edge stopped by their dorm room. She said "Hi" to both of them, but looked at and talked more often to Davis. Andrew didn't like it.

After the young lady left, Davis excused himself to go to the bathroom. I watched Andrew snoop through Davis's high school yearbook before he returned. When he flipped through the sports section he whispered, "A crew team . . . his school had a lot of money." As he read a few signed quotes from some of Davis's classmates, he said, "Oh interesting . . . they're a little wild . . . and worldly." As soon as Andrew heard Davis walking back into the room he put the yearbook down and picked up his Bible.

Andrew doesn't seem to like the quickness of Davis's mind, and he grows anxious as Davis's popularity increases. Last night at The Edge's first social event, Andrew noticed several students gathering around Davis. He then jumped into their conversation and said, "Oh, hey, Davis, I forgot to mention that a couple of your friends stopped by our room. They said they've been out several nights in a row. They um . . . invited you to a party tonight. Guys from your high school. One of them was pretty drunk. Just wanted to share before I forgot."

Davis gave Andrew a look, like he was surprised at what he was hearing, but the next second he smiled and shrugged his shoulders. "They must have been confused, bro," he said. "I didn't hang out with people like that in high school."

The rest of the group looked around at each other until one of them changed the subject to talk about the upcoming football game. But as Andrew and Davis walked home together, I watched Andrew drill Davis with questions about his background.

"So, were those guys who came by your good friends?"

"I don't know who they were. You didn't get any names?"

"Did you drink a lot in high school?" Andrew asked.

"No, not at all. I came to Christ my sophomore year and made some good friends at youth group. None of us drank."

"Sophomore year? Are you . . . from a Christian home?"

"I grew up in church and my family are believers," Davis answered. "But I never really owned it when I was younger. Jesus became real and personal to me my sophomore year."

"I see," Andrew said. He didn't say much for the rest of the walk home.

Davis hasn't been naive of Andrew's opinion of him. After a couple of similar conversations in the first few days, Davis sensed tension and humbly approached Andrew about it.

"Andrew, are we okay? We're going to be living together all year, and I kind of feel like there might be something between us we need to talk through?"

"Something like what, Davis?"

"I don't know. It seems like you might be upset with me or uncomfortable around me sometimes."

"No, not me. It's all good," Andrew said. He then quickly changed the subject and asked about Davis's English class.

This pains me to see. And to complicate matters, Andrew has been appointed to a leadership position in The Edge, the very ministry Davis plans on joining. Andrew has been reading announcements from the microphone at the beginning of the ministry's gatherings. I wonder how this will sit with Davis.

The tension between the two of them also puzzles me. It doesn't seem to me as though Davis did anything to Andrew, so why are Satan's minions so easily able to incite a rivalry between them?

Most respectfully your humble servant,
Littleton (Hereafter *L*)

August 30

Littleton,

Competition runs deep through the veins of American culture. Every time Davis leaves his dorm room he faces a sea of people, mostly peers, who compete with him on various levels. In his current situation it is primarily social competition and positioning as each young man struggles to find his place. Their rivalries begin in high school but escalate during the college and young professional years, when every young man is vying to make his mark. Men chiefly desire respect. Remember this as you deal with Davis, and it will guide you well.

Andrew's envy may weigh on Davis's mind when he hears Andrew talk from the microphone before ministry gatherings. Consequently, Davis could have a difficult time worshipping there. So our enemy's tactic—and it is an effective one—is aimed to cut Davis off from the worshipping community of his school friends and hall mates. All of this is an attempt to make him turn away from our Lord.

> *"Wrath is cruel, anger is overwhelming,*
> *but who can stand before jealousy?"*
> *(Proverbs 27:4)*

Encourage him throughout the day, and help him cultivate a forgiving spirit as quickly as you can so he doesn't carry a grudge. And keep me posted about relationship tensions of any type. Let me know right away if they start talking behind each other's backs.

And by the way, the mission trip was no accident. I've learned through an intelligence report that Jesus hand-picked Pastor Peter from Kenya to influence Davis. Pastor Peter grew up in a village of dire poverty and disease. And yet he learned to trust the Father when circumstances seemed hopeless. Christ used the tool of adversity to forge radiant joy in his spirit. He has tremendous spiritual power and he's spurred on many young leaders over the years. Anticipate strong resistance from the Enemy–they'll probably try to block Davis from going on this mission trip at all costs.

AM

September 3

Archangel Michael,

Relationship conflicts continue. Fallen angels are working hard to make Davis feel isolated in his dorm community. They made another strike yesterday. Davis and Andrew had been temporarily living in a three-person dorm room alone, but they have now been assigned a third roommate, a student named Mark Todley. Mark spends a minimum of five hours a day in front of the TV; he is socially disconnected and extremely guarded. Watching him play video games, I can see it's his way to fantasize about being a hero, to feel a sense of worth or accomplishment. And I can tell it's beginning to wear on Davis. Davis really hoped to get someone he liked. I heard it in his voice as he talked over the phone to Jonathan.

"God's at work in our mission trip! Several parents and leaders in the church jumped in with support. We're eighty percent funded!" Jonathan said.

"Wow, that's great!"

"I know. I can't believe it. Hey, how are things with Andrew?"

"About the same. I don't really trust him so we don't talk much. But we're getting a third roommate. That should help."

Of course, with Mark, Davis didn't get what he hoped for. Here's a brief excerpt of a conversation from this afternoon, when Davis stopped at the doorway of Mark's room:

"Hey, what's up?"

"Nothing," Mark said, not taking his eyes off the TV screen.

"Some guys are headed to the gym to shoot some hoops later if you want to join us."

This comment met dead silence as Mark kept playing video games. Davis tried once again to strike up a conversation.

"How's math going?"

"Good," Mark said, still glued to the screen.

A similar pattern repeats itself. Mark gives one- or two-word answers to send Davis the signal he doesn't want to get to know him or to be known by him. Davis grows lonelier by the day.

The other guys on the floor don't offer much in the way of friendship, either. The room on the left houses two students who openly show pornography and have drawn several others on their floor to watch it with them. Davis's roommate, Mark, has a similar addiction to porn, but he keeps it a secret and hasn't joined in with the others. On the right is the men's bathroom.

In the meantime, I am getting to know Davis better each day. Yesterday afternoon he stopped into the bookstore and purchased four notebooks, two binders, one clipboard, three different-colored highlight markers, and one pack of legal pads of paper. He is a minimalist—he purchased precisely what he needed and no more, and he aimed to keep his backpack light.

It rained that day. And it rained today. Many students studied in their dorm rooms. But Davis seemed to have difficulty concentrating, with Andrew constantly looking for his faults and Mark playing video games. So Davis walked across campus both days and studied in the library. He gazed out the window and appeared to be in low spirits. Davis then opened his notebook and sketched a long hallway with many doors. He wrote "#206" on one of the doors. From observing this, I gathered that for Davis his dorm room feels more like a hotel room to check into at night rather than a place he can call home. The moment spoke volumes to me. Seeking to lift his spirits, I reminded Davis of one of his favorite songs and he reached into his pocket, pulled out his phone, and played it. By the smile it brought to his face, I'd say it was effective.

L

September 6

Littleton,

A report came to me yesterday. Our angelic warriors have been facing overwhelming numbers at a time when prayer petitions from campus have been at an all-time low. Our senior commanders send troubling news:

> Monday, September 3rd, 2:00 p.m.: Opposition by enemy forces was formidable as they traversed westward and captured the Northern Bank.

> Tuesday, September 4th, 3:00 p.m.: Their numbers nearly doubled. In the onslaught, my horse was attacked and severely injured; no longer of use in this battle.

> Tuesday, September 5th, 8:00 p.m.: Our platoon regrouped to regional headquarters to see if any additional prayer support had come our way. The report came back negative. Nearly everyone on campus has gone in search of fleeting pleasure, turning from the God of their youth.

Based on my experience in similar environments, the bloodbath will continue and only grow more severe. A spiritual attack is coming your way soon. You need to plan for the worst. How can we minimize damage and hold the line until things get better? After much reflection, I started to think that, if possible, it might be best if we could reinforce Davis's faith through influences within his very dorm hall. A couple of connections, maybe even just one, to stem the tide.

He's going to need reinforcements–and by that I mean people–students of solid Christian character who can counteract discouragements aimed at turning him from the Lord. Look everywhere, but I suggest you start first in his dorm hall.

AM

September 9

Archangel Michael,

> "... do not give the devil a foothold." Ephesians 4:27 (NIV)

Oh, my. I'm starting to watch this verse play out in Davis's life. The past two weeks he's spent a lot of time attending fraternity rush events, and he's headed down a narrow and largely secular road. I have discovered a few true Christians in his social circles, but every time I try to make an introduction, several demons rush in and block me by getting between me and the students. This gets frustrating. I fight with everything I have to break through their group, but I'm simply outnumbered.

Cut off from spiritual community and close friendships, Davis is now beginning to drift away from God. The steady, unrelenting currents of roommate tensions, dorm isolation, and religious hypocrisy have untied the ropes that bound him to shore, and the ripples of college popularity and status are beginning to carry him out to sea.

Three or four of the big houses are aggressively pursuing him, and he's enjoying the attention. The Chi house, in particular, is sending their most influential members to take him out for steak dinners. It's one of the historically popular, old row fraternities with a gorgeous building masking what seems to be a spiritually dark place.

Here's an example from dinner, where Warren and Grant, two seniors from the Chi fraternity, sat with Davis at an upscale, casual steak house. A waiter approached their table, took their drink orders, and then asked: "Are you gentlemen interested in an appetizer?"

Warren took the lead. "We'll take two orders of the shrimp appetizer." He turned to Davis and said, "They have excellent shrimp here."

"The grilled calamari, too," Grant said.

Warren asked Davis, "Do you see anything else?"

Davis, laughing under his breath, said, "I think that'll probably be enough guys. Thanks."

Then the waiter said, "Our stuffed portobello mushrooms are probably our bestseller."

"Sure, bring them as well," said Warren, waving his hand. "And bring that olive oil you have–the one with truffle in it."

I leaned in and whispered from Psalm 12:2, *"With flattering lips, and with a double heart do they speak."*

As the waiter walked away, Grant turned to Davis. "Hope you don't mind that we ordered the appetizers for you. I know not everyone likes seafood."

"Oh, I love seafood," Davis said. "My family spends part of our summers at my grandfather's place in Charleston, so we eat a lot of it."

Warren and Grant glanced at each other, and then Grant asked, "Where's his place?"

"Isle of Palms."

"No way! Is your family from Charleston?" Grant asked.

"My dad's side is."

"Nice. Hey, Grant's parents have a beach house on Tybee Island. It's one of our favorite trips. "

Grant took a sip of his sweet tea and then said, "We go every Spring–a bunch of us."

"Yeah, remember last year? When Harrison . . . "

Warren turned to Davis and said, "One of our graduating seniors was pretty drunk, and he started streaking down the beach one night."

Grant and Warren laughed, but they kept their eyes on Davis. So much so that I sensed they were trying to gauge his reaction to see if he would join in.

Davis smiled. "No way. What'd you guys do?"

"What could we do? We just laughed about it. Can't tell a drunk guy what to do."

"No kidding," Davis said. He took a sip of his water and unfolded his napkin. "Were girls around?"

"None of our girls. He was mostly running by people we didn't know."

"I guess he was kind of, um, making new friends, huh?" Davis said, which made them laugh more.

This is when I leaned in to whisper from Proverbs 15:2, *"The mouth of fools spouts folly."*

As the laughs started to die down, Davis asked, "That does sound crazy. Is it like that all the time?"

"Kinda," Grant said. "Something wild usually happens when we all get together, especially at the beach. Like that one time when Hudson–"

Warren cut him off. "So how many weeks do you spend at Isle of Palms in the summer?"

"Depends on the year," Davis said, "and what else is going on. Last summer it was only two. I had a couple of lacrosse camps, and our youth group's summer camp in Florida."

"So great, man. Sounds like an awesome summer," Warren said.

"Yeah, it really was."

Davis excused himself to wash his hands before the food arrived. After he got up from the table and walked towards the restroom, Warren said, "What do you think about him?"

"I like him, man. Seems a little straight, but he'll grow out of that."

"Me too. I think he's perfect." Warren looked down at his phone. "The Forrester's party is in two weeks. Maybe we just need to tell him he's getting a bid."

"You know we can't do that. It's against the rules."

"Who cares? We gotta get him."

"Warren, we can't."

"Well, then, let's just *hint* at it. We can tell him about the Forrester's casino night."

"I . . . I don't think that's a good idea. We're supposed to talk to Marshall first."

"Look, we'll find out how much he likes us. And just let me take it from there. Cool?"

"Yeah," Grant said, playing with his straw. "I guess so."

When Davis returned to the table, Warren jumped right in. "So we never got to ask you how Rush has been going."

"It's been good."

"How do you like our house? Do you have any questions about it?"

"I think you guys are great. I'm just wondering who else is rushing, and what, you know, they're like. I'm trying to find the house I fit into the best."

Warren nodded. "Sure. I get it. Hey, do you know the Forrester family?"

"Not offhand, no."

"They're strong alumni supporters here in town, and they have an amazing place near Silver Lakes. Every year they throw an annual casino smoker event."

"I've heard of that night. Some of my friends going through Rush have been talking about it."

"Yeah, it's great. Invitations don't officially go out until next week. But between us" . . . Warren leaned in slightly . . . "you're going to get one."

"Hey, thanks!"

"And at the party you'll meet the other rushees we feel strongly about. We'll have narrowed down to our final thirty. And we'll be sharing our social calendar for the year with you guys."

"Everyone really likes you, man," Grant said.

"Thanks. I like you guys, too."

Archangel Michael, I'm concerned.

L

September 10

Archangel Michael,

Davis is drawn to the Chi house because it is the same fraternity his father joined, which makes Davis a "legacy." Here's part of the phone conversation he had with his father last night, when they discussed Rush:

"What's the latest with Rush?"

"It's going well," Davis said, giving his father a general overview of the houses he's rushing. Then, when he got to his father's fraternity he said, "They mentioned the reference letters you wrote for me. Thanks for that. They seemed impressed."

"Oh, that's great. That was the idea. But I want you to go where you feel comfortable."

"Thanks. I know. I've narrowed my choices down to three houses. We're two weeks away from receiving bids."

"That's exciting. Let's catch up after this weekend when you go through your next round of parties."

"Definitely," Davis said before they hung up.

Davis could probably tell from his father's tone that he hopes Davis will continue the family legacy. Mr. Chandler sent several reference letters to campus before Davis arrived, but only to his own fraternity. He didn't ask any of his friends to send references to any of the other houses.

Students like this house, too. Many of Davis's peers are enamored with the attention he's receiving. This campus is steeped in tradition, so I think it will be hard for Davis to break from the expected path of both his family and friends. And given his loneliness in the dorm there doesn't seem to be much of a dilemma in his mind about heading this way.

In contrast to this frustrating dorm room experience, he'll have a pledge class of about thirty friends, a big brother, and introductions to an entire network of sorority girls. Davis also knows he will walk across campus wearing fraternity letters that will cause students' heads to turn. He will have made it to the elite, the very center of action on campus.

When you are outside in the heat of summer, shouldn't you jump into the cool body of water lying in front of you? Never mind that the pool might be toxic.

L

September 11

Archangel Michael,

The Chi's are tapping into something deep within Davis. Today Warren and Grant stopped to talk to him on campus. Several demons hovered in the air, and two of them entered into the students as the conversation began.

"Hey Davis, let's catch up early next week. Carlton is taking us to the Marsh Creek Plantation this weekend to go shooting," Warren said.

"Oh, that sounds great! A group of seniors?"

"Yeah, mostly. But no worries, we'll do it again. We usually do a larger trip in the spring."

"Yeah? Is that right?"

"Yeah," Grant said, "And we have a low-country boil that night. We actually pay a professional photographer to shoot the weekend. You'll see pictures blown up in some of our rooms. It's a time to get off campus and let loose a bit."

Davis smiled and said, "Hey, I look forward to seeing 'em." He then watched them wave to two extremely attractive girls across campus.

Archangel Michael, I've noticed these guys talk with calculated ambiguity. When they referred to the Tybee Island trip at dinner, they said, "Something wild usually happens." And now they say they're going to "let loose a bit," which could mean smoke cigars or it could mean heroin. We don't know from the surface. But I think they're testing Davis's tolerance for partying. And while they're doing this, they're closing in.

I'm having a hard time competing. Davis's notion of college ministry is thus far dominated by a vision of Andrew talking at the microphone, while our enemies offer the very center of the university's elite. He is becoming overly concerned with his reputation on campus and is tying his identity too closely to Greek life. With all of this activity, Davis is becoming too busy for Jesus and too distracted to earnestly seek a faith community; his sinful pride has been piqued and now it craves more and more attention.

How can we overturn this enormous social pressure? Can there be a way for Davis to "live in this world, but not of it" in this sort of environment? Or does he need to completely withdraw from these circles?

L

September 12

Littleton,

What you are experiencing is one of the worst parts of our assignments and among the most difficult to watch. Allow me to give you some history. Over the years, the fraternity you expressed concern about has pledged several former students from Davis's high school. Yes, steak dinners with the wealthiest guys on campus certainly feel good when you're looking for friends, but you're right, there's real danger here. Drug dealers are eyeing that house; there's a lot of money there. The Chi's actually have a small but growing group of brothers who are heavy cocaine users.

Of course, they don't talk about anything like that during Rush. They just dress well and smoke cigars. Then they go to each other's lake and farm houses on the weekend and "let loose." Brilliant little marketers, all of them. But not a lick of redemption is happening in that place. They are a group of students whose hearts are closed to the Lord. It's an ambush, Littleton. Fallen angels abound.

So . . . since our enemies are starting to gain significant ground I petitioned for increased reinforcements. And I learned you will deliver an important angelic message tomorrow. The note from our Lord said: "Make sure Davis gets a haircut this week from a Mr. Robert Phillips."

I look forward to watching your delivery method.

AM

September 14

Littleton,

Nice delivery. Clever move to have one of the Chi members point out the barber shop to Davis. I enjoyed watching you steer Davis to enter the shop just as Robert rang up a client at the front desk register. You fulfilled the first part of our assignment. You simply must make sure Davis follows through with his appointment and does not get sidetracked.

Why is getting a haircut from Mr. Phillips such a big deal? Robert John Phillips grew up with seven siblings and comes from a family lineage that has six generations of ministers. On his mother's side they are relatives of the minister R. L. Dabney, who was the chaplain to Stonewall Jackson during his Shenandoah campaign in the Civil War. Robert's father currently serves as the pastor of a medium-sized church twenty miles from the city as the crow flies. He has been in that position for seventeen years. Money was fairly tight for the Phillips family of ten, but they are all well instructed in the faith. As a child, Robert always knew four things about his parents:

- They both dearly loved Jesus.
- They were deeply in love and had a lot of fun together.
- They lived simply (some would say frugally) to ensure that their children had the best education.
- They had, or at least appeared to have, no preference for what extracurricular activities their kids chose during school, nor what career paths they took. They only asked them to consider how they were designed by God, and then to use their gifts for His Glory.

Early in life Robert felt a calling to the Gospel Ministry, but having grown up as a preacher's kid he had neither the interest nor the desire to seek ordination. But one thing Robert did know; he was keenly interested in how God works through everyday conversations. He longed to work in an environment where he would be face-to-face with people.

Robert considered teaching as a profession, but then a little while later thought about a retail environment. Two major influences helped shape his decision to become a barber. First, he noticed his barber had a direct means of connecting with all sorts of people in a way ministers and teachers don't. Second, his best friend's father owned a retail men's clothing line, and he learned much from the numerous retail conversations he heard in their family's living room.

Upon graduating from high school, Robert enrolled in a one-year biblical studies and pastoral counseling course at the local seminary. As you might expect, biblical studies came easily to him but counseling was a new venture, and he became deeply interested in how the two interrelated.

In one of his pastoral counseling courses, Robert became acquainted with a Mary Jane Harrison, who at the time was a fellow student working in a Christian retail store and trying to build up some college credits. Mary Jane received the highest marks in her classes and often had a line of people approaching her after class, seeking her advice. She was also beautiful, and as soon as Robert received the first inkling that Mary Jane might be interested in him he asked her out on a date. They married exactly one year later. She is, to this day, his best friend and wisest counselor.

After his one-year program was over, Robert needed help launching his career. Through a series of conversations, events, and much diligent prayer, he felt almost pressed upon by the Lord to start a traditional men's barbershop. He then worked for a few years learning his craft and saving up money to build his own shop. By now, year after year he has worked as an expert barber, but more importantly, he has spent much time memorizing biblical Proverbs and learning the art of conversation.

The shop you see today has a vintage designed locker room in the back where barbers can hang their coats. Robert had it built to reflect the university stadiums where athletes suit up before stepping out to the field. At the top of his locker, there is a black rectangular magnet with white block letters. Two words: "On mission."

When Robert receives a first-time client he always touches base with the person about their family, upbringing, and current life situation. In so doing he tactfully finds out about their relationship with the Lord. His memory is like a steel trap. He prays for his customers' well-being and that Jesus would give him the right words to say during sessions. Robert is well acquainted with the spiritual currents of the town and the university; he even knows a fair bit about the student ministry groups on campus. He knows all of the spiritually strong churches in the area and, over time, has picked up connections across the city.

Through Robert's barber chair, God has built up exceptionally well-rooted families and helped restore several broken marriages. He has groomed two senators, ten entrepreneurs, and twenty-two consultants. He has called many to the pulpit, and He has spawned a host of literary writers. He has also, through a rather interesting turn of events, helped to orchestrate circumstances so that many young couples find their way to the altar.

Robert has one primary spiritual skill—he is exceptionally adept at recognizing God's movements through the everyday affairs of his clients. Consequently, the most practical advice in the city (and often the wisest) passes through the barber's shop.

Robert's shop is a beacon of light for this city, and it may be the light that breaks through Davis's darkness.

AM

September 17

Archangel Michael,

Robert is great! And I found all your statements about how well he interacts with people to be true. Davis immediately felt comfortable with him and opened up in a way I haven't seen him do since I started this assignment. I wish I could relay all that went on during his first haircut with Robert, but for the sake of brevity, I'll share some key takeaways.

Through their conversation, Davis came to realize that he might need to leave The Edge and seek out another student ministry. "During worship I try . . . I really try to forget about how Andrew drives me nuts . . . "

Robert jumped in at the pause. "Kind of hard to worship when you feel like one of the leaders is working against you. Roommate or not. That stuff gets in your head."

"Yeah, it does."

"Anytime you find yourself fighting mind battles–you know, rewinding the tape, replaying bad conversations–you can bet the enemy is up to something."

Davis didn't say anything. But he stopped looking at the TV.

"Forgiveness and finding another group might be your best options here," Robert said while patting Davis on the shoulder.

Later in the haircut, Robert gave Davis some further advice, this time on viewing his student involvement and choice of majors as a calling.

"Don't just do what's popular or take the quickest path to making money. Jesus might call you there, but He might not. What do you love? What are you good at? What are you gifted in? Most important, where does He want you? With what student groups? And who can be your real friends, ones who can really sharpen you in the Lord?"

Davis didn't answer Robert's questions, appearing to mull over them instead. I could tell by the way he blinked in rhythm to the snipping of Robert's shears that his mind was actively at work.

Davis went back to his dorm room that night and found Mark and Andrew gone. He picked up his Bible and read the inscription written from his former youth minister:

"Davis, stay with the Lord and read this Book."

He then walked over to the bed, lay down on his stomach and propped the Bible on his pillow. When he opened it, I had him turn to Isaiah 40:31:

> " . . . but they who wait for the Lord shall renew their strength;
> they shall mount up with wings like eagles; they shall run and
> not be weary; they shall walk and not faint."

Davis clenched his right fist and shook it up and down. I can tell that this verse strengthened him.

I also popped into his mind a memory of his friend Jonathan. Davis immediately picked up the phone and called him. Jonathan responded with joy when he heard Davis's voice.

"How are you, bro? What's new on campus?"

After some small talk about classes, Fraternity Rush, and some of the people he's been meeting, Davis said, "I really miss you and the youth group. I'm still struggling to find friends."

"So . . . the roommate situation?"

"No better."

"Any luck with people in the student ministry?"

"Not really. Andrew's always around. I can't stand listening to him from the microphone. It all feels fake. Shallow. I think the Lord may want me to move on and find another ministry."

Jonathan was quiet for a long moment, and I could feel a renewal of strength as he sent up a silent prayer for Davis. He then continued.

"That's probably wise. Look, I'm sorry it's not working out for you at The Edge. But try not to harbor anger or bitterness against Andrew. It'll just bring you down. Easier said than done. I know that."

"Yeah, yeah. You're right."

"God's got something good for you. He loves you, brother. Don't forget it!"

"Thanks, man. I wish you were here."

"Me too. Hey, I've got an idea. Remember that sermon from Drew Hamilton from Charleston? He talked about how when we have times in our lives where we don't have anyone to talk to, we simply work it out with God and stay connected to Him, even when we don't feel anything. He said, 'Sing to the Lord. Worship Him deeply. And trust He will bring us friends in His good timing.' I've got it on video. I'll send it to you."

"Thanks. I would really appreciate that."

So the day ended well. When Davis hung up the phone he was visibly encouraged. His whole countenance lifted, and he was smiling. I'm searching diligently to find another Jonathan on this campus.

L

September 20

Archangel Michael,

Warren and Grant from the Chi fraternity knocked on Davis's door. When he opened it, they greeted him with friendly smiles and small-talked about how his week was going before saying, "So, here's your tickets to the Forrester's casino smoker." They then presented Davis with a sealed, monogrammed envelope containing two tickets.

I've learned that the casino smoker is an annual charity fundraiser that takes place at the Forrester's, a house that backs up to Silver Lakes Country Club and has a stunning view of the thirteenth hole. The Forresters are big fraternity alumni donors and have the party every year to coincide with fall rush. It's a party Davis's peers are talking about, many of whom would trade nearly anything for an invitation.

And then Davis did something neither the seniors nor (I'll admit) I anticipated–he declined their invitation.

"Thanks guys, but I'm gonna pass," Davis told them, handing back the tickets. "I've thought about it. I'm not interested in pledging with you."

His comments met with blank stares on each of the seniors' faces.

"Nothing personal; I just don't feel like it's the direction I'm headed. But y'all have fun!"

Shocked, after an awkward pause Grant said, "Okay. Good luck. See you around."

Davis did this without yet receiving a bid from another house, nor any other social guarantees. After he closed the door he picked up a copy of an invitation from a different fraternity–one I heard Davis describe as "a well-liked house girls speak highly of"–and set it on his desk, throwing all other Greek invitations and student organization literature away. He then put on his running shoes and headphones and took off for the track.

I was shocked, and I can't wait to tell the other angels! Davis has been drifting from Christ, but this showed me there is still faith inside him, some parts hard as steel. For all his struggles this semester, connecting with Robert gave him enough strength to resist the cultural pressure. I can see that Davis wants respect from his peers, but at least right now he wants Jesus more.

Satan's minions had a fit. And they've come back raging.

The war is on.

L

September 20

Dear Littleton,

Big gain! You helped resist the attack! Privileged environments are tough terrain. Even our strongest believers can become swayed when placed in positions of social power. As soon as humility fades they lose their spiritual compass. Yet our Father is patient with His children. He knows their frailties and He knows how easily they can be distracted. We're to look at Davis similarly to how Michelangelo looked at a blank marble slab. He didn't see mere stone; he saw hidden potential. And he worked diligently and patiently to reveal it.

Incidentally, what we're experiencing is typical of our enemies' attacks. They surround a believer with social pressures from several angles. Through events and circumstances they temporarily cut off connections to other Christians, so the person feels alone and starts to doubt the presence (and goodness) of God. During this time the believer is blinded to God's providence.

The Encourager says to keep on fighting and get ready for an increased surge from the Enemy. Stay focused on bringing Davis relationships. And keep working on renewing his mind.

AM

September 21

Archangel Michael,

They're using Andrew's envy to wear Davis down. Two weeks ago, after The Edge, a group of students went out to dinner and sat outside on large picnic tables. After ordering his meal, Davis walked over and sat next to Andrew to join his conversation, which surprised me because he usually keeps his distance. He may have been trying to build a bridge. Andrew, however, continued talking to those around him and didn't acknowledge Davis. He adjusted his seating position to lean his back toward Davis, as though subtly attempting to block him out of their conversation. Andrew was at the center of the conversation, talking about The Edge ministry:

"Next weekend? Leadership retreat for The Edge," said Andrew.

"Where are y'all going?" Davis asked Andrew, trying to join in.

"Oh, we rented a house on Lake Sebastian." Andrew then resumed his same posture of leaning toward the others.

When Davis got up to refill his drink, Andrew watched him leave the table. As soon as Davis got out of speaking distance, Andrew turned back to the others.

"Y'all are welcome to come up to our barbecue on Sunday afternoon. It's a sweet property. We'll have a volleyball net and a swimming pool, and a dock by the lake."

When Davis returned to the table, Andrew didn't invite him to the barbecue. Davis later found out he didn't get invited, confirming Andrew's envy. He's been attending worship nights at The Edge less frequently ever since.

L

September 23

Archangel Michael,

More of the same. Yesterday Andrew and two other guys I recognized from The Edge crossed paths with Davis on campus. The four of them chatted for a few minutes.

One of the guys asked Davis, "Where have you been? We miss seeing you at The Edge."

Davis deflected the question. "I know. I've been busy."

Andrew remained silent, but after Davis walked away he turned to the other student and said, "I've been doing everything I can to be a positive influence on him. We need to keep praying for Davis."

When Davis got out of earshot from Andrew and the other student, he called Jonathan. "I'm having a hard time. It's Andrew."

"Still, huh? Tell me about it."

"He invited a bunch of people to an Edge barbecue but never told me about it. He's annoying to live with because he talks a lot about Jesus, but he doesn't live that way. And when he speaks from the microphone during ministry gatherings, he just seems so fake."

"So sorry, bro. Do most of your Christian friends go to The Edge?"

"Yeah."

"I bet that's hard."

"Really hard. I hate it when they ask me why I don't come more often. Their faces light up when they talk about the ministry, and I don't want to be that person who complains about it. I end up saying something like, 'I know, I should go more often,' but I really feel like telling them I can't stand hearing Andrew from the microphone."

Davis sighed and then continued. "To say that, though, would mean I'd have to talk bad about Andrew behind his back. And I don't feel right about that, either."

"Hmmm. That's rough. What about another student ministry?"

43

"Yeah, I've just . . . been busy. Haven't really had time to look."

"Well, if I can offer some advice here, I'd tell you to make it a priority. You need to be spiritually fed, you know?"

"Yeah, I know," Davis said, and then he turned the conversation a different direction by asking Jonathan what he'd been up to lately.

Later that night, Davis returned to his dorm room only to find Mark playing video games, unwilling to talk to him. When Andrew arrived he avoided Davis except for making a passing comment about an upcoming retreat, noting how "everyone is growing so close together." It seemed he was, at least in part, seeking to undermine Davis. It hurts me to watch all this.

I am doing a lot of encouraging–popping Scripture passages and good memories into his mind, and keeping him in touch with his family and high school friends. All of these messages help to lift his spirits, but I want to do more than merely react to the Accuser's tactics. I can't help but feel like this is a tennis match, with joy and hope on our side volleying against the fear and discouragement that have taken root in Davis's heart. Only there's way more of them on their side of the court. I want to lead this fight, not follow. But they have such a stronghold here. I'm wondering how we can be more effective at this point in time as Davis doesn't have a community of strong believers or much prayer support to prop him up.

I very much look forward to your reply.

L

September 28

Dear Littleton,

That's the hard part of this battle. It all depends on Davis's heart. The closer he turns to the Father, the more resources you'll get. In the meantime, stay focused on reminding Davis of God's goodness so he can trust Him more. Our enemies will do whatever they can to manipulate and distort his views.

Keep fighting; you're doing great! We knew this would be a difficult environment. Let me know how relationship tensions affect Davis's prayer life.

AM

October 1

Archangel Michael,

The frustration keeps gnawing at him. Last night he awoke in the middle of the night and he couldn't get back to sleep. He lay on his back, restless. And after an hour he finally turned to prayer

"Jesus, where are you? Why don't you help me? I feel so alone here. Doesn't seem like you care. I know what Andrew's like. I can't stand listening to him from the microphone on Tuesday nights. It just . . . it makes the whole ministry seem like, like a joke. I can't believe they picked him. And now Mark. What's wrong with him? He never wants to talk. He doesn't even say "Hi." Nothing. Just stays glued to the video games. Not how I envisioned college. I'm lonely, Lord. I'm feeling restless. Why won't you help me? Did I do something wrong? Come on, God. All I can do is keep coming to you and asking for more help. But when I do, things seem to get worse. Like now. I can't even sleep. This is frustrating. I'm trying not to turn my back on you God, but how can I not?"

It was a raw, unadulterated prayer. Sheer honesty, just like the Psalms. I drew close and strengthened him by whispering "God will never leave you" into his mind. This calmed his emotions so he could rest.

All the best,

L

October 2

Littleton,

On returning to my war strategy room last night I put down my sword and opened my trunk only to discover a package of correspondence. When I saw your letter it brought a smile to my face. Always great to hear from you, Littleton.

Loneliness and occasional sleepless nights touch all of God's people. Davis is experiencing the standard warfare of this culture-discouragement, isolation, frustration. Count on these tactics of the Deceiver to resurface time and again. Our enemies can't create anything new; all they can do is try to manipulate given situations to stir up strife.

Since Jesus is allowing these things to happen to Davis, He has a better plan around the corner and it doesn't seem like connecting with The Edge is part of it. The love of Christ is strategic beyond our ability to comprehend. I've been on assignments where what seems that the most trivial, humdrum life events or decisions turn out to be the hinges, the very turning points, for the rest of people's lives, impacting generations to come.

> "The heart of man plans his ways, but the Lord establishes his steps." (Proverbs 16:9)

Littleton, when this assignment first came to me, our King of Kings shared that you've been endowed with an exceptional capacity to discern the intricacies of human personality, to strip through the layers of flesh and see who people are deep down at their core. The assignment ended with the following sentence:

"Littleton has an eye for detail that is pure genius."

Let's hone your skills right away. We need you to know Davis well and respond quickly to life situations as they arise. Please send me a letter capturing another moment in time–an instance in which Davis's actions reflect what is spiritually going on inside him. Then offer commentary and describe how you responded to him. This gives me a chance to see how you interpret interactions and intervene, so I can help streamline your efforts and sharpen your skills.

I also need you to pay special attention to whatever resonates with him. Jesus will always operate through Davis's primary passions–the tendencies of his mind, the preferences he exhibits, the gifts he has been given. These are what make up the person and assign to him a place in life where he can truly be a shining light for Christ. And this is where you can best reach him.

AM

October 4

Archangel Michael,

Davis went shopping for clothes today. Per your request, I've taken close note of his actions and offered my commentary and reactions below. Here's a copy of Davis's retail sales receipt and a brief excerpt of his conversation with the salesman.

Pair of Shorts	1	$70
Tweed Sport Coat	1	$750
Pair of Suspenders	2	$110
Pair of Socks	2	$25
Bow tie	1	$65

His conversation with the salesman went as follows.

"Try on this sport coat."

Davis tried it on. "I really like it. It's sharp." He looked at the pile of clothes he'd already been considering. "But it's still warm outside. And I already have a tweed coat."

"This one just came in; no one's seen it yet. Notice the pattern. Hand stitched, then tailored to an athletic fit."

"Wow, I do really like the fit." Davis looked at it from several angles in the mirror.

"We've told our supplier in New York we need younger, slightly more aggressive options."

"I'll take it. Thanks," said Davis as he put the coat down and reached for his wallet. "I'm really glad I found this store."

My commentary: This is a traditional men's clothing shop, probably similar to one he and his father would have frequented in Georgia. It troubles me that Davis bought a tweed jacket even though it's still shorts weather, and paid full price for it. This purchase, combined with the fact that he's been to this store three times in the last two weeks, reinforces his loneliness and lack of community. The store reminds him of home. It's an attempt to cover up internal pain.

So, since I thought he was in low spirits and trying to prop himself up, I brought back a memory of him and his high school youth group friends floating down a river in inner tubes. It seemed to lift his spirits.

I think part of Davis's anxiety stems from how taxing it is to go through Fraternity Rush. Most of the conversations he's having with other students are superficial, and many of his peers talk about nothing else. Davis enjoys these conversations for a while, because he likes having his finger on the pulse of his surroundings, but he longs for more depth. Sometimes he leaves a large social event to walk off alone.

L

October 8

Littleton,

Excellent detail. I knew you were quick.

As long as Davis has a heart for the Lord there will come a day when his inner spirit shines brighter than his new clothing, when he awakens, set ablaze by the Spirit and focused on higher things, when his joy overpowers fear and loneliness and he walks regularly with a solid community of believers. A day when we are on the offensive, no longer casting our energy towards minimizing damage. We can then attack and force our enemies to respond to situations we ourselves have created. We will hold onto the hope that, by God's grace and with the turn of a few pivotal moments, that day can come soon.

Spend as much of your time as you can trying to find a connection for him. Someone with whom he can really let down his guard. Someone who will encourage him in the Lord. Perhaps somebody new, someone he's not yet met. Littleton, he can't win without a friend.

"Iron sharpens iron, and one man sharpens another."
(Proverbs 27:17)

AM

October 30

Archangel Michael,

Davis pledged Sigma fraternity, a big name house of extremely well-liked guys.

To give you a window into his social world, let me tell you about the game on Saturday, the first home football game weekend. Great fun on campus, though several spiritual landmines had been planted that Davis had to avoid just to keep walking straight. A group of guys on Davis's dorm approached him on Friday.

"Hey, Davis, join us for breakfast club tomorrow morning. 7 a.m. Three large boxes of Cheerios and a fifth of tequila." The guys laughed.

Davis laughed as well, but then he said, "No thanks, I have a mixer to go to before the game. But I'll see you guys soon."

I really liked watching the way Davis handled this–the way he refused their offer, but kept up a relationship with them. Davis met his pledge class on Saturday morning to clean up their fraternity house before the football game fire-up party. Kickoff was at 11:00 a.m. But approximately one-third of Davis's pledge class skipped the game to play a drinking game. The remaining pledges (Davis included) went to the stadium and cheered on the team in the warm sunshine.

Davis ended up standing near a young lady named Elizabeth, whom he talked with throughout the game. He knew her from one of his classes, so they were not strangers. One of Davis's pledge brothers described Elizabeth as "beautiful, the girl most guys want, and wealthy too." From my observations at the game, it looks like the two of them may be spending some time together in the future.

"So, hey, have you thought much about that project? The one for marketing?" Elizabeth said.

"Nope. That's still a ways off. Have you?"

"I have a few ideas. It would be pretty easy to make it a retail case study. Maybe, I don't know, do you want to . . . meet up sometime and I can tell you my thoughts?"

"Sure. I'll give you my number."

After their football team won, Davis, Elizabeth, and some others went to the University Spirit shop and bought the latest Greek lettered t-shirts and polos. As they left the store, Elizabeth said, "I can't wait to wear these. Everyone will recognize these letters from a mile away."

Fraternity life has ushered in lots of excitement, and for Davis it seems to be a welcome social outlet to counteract the Dorm Hall blues. His spiritual drift, however, continues. For the last several weeks of Fraternity Rush, all of life has been centered on him. Davis has been considered an insider, and popular upperclassmen have waited on him nearly hand-and-foot. Oblivious to what's been happening, he has been experiencing a great shift–from a life-orientation of serving God and others toward one of gratifying self.

Self-inflated pride fights to capture his spirit through everyday events. It is a silent, subtle take-over Davis cannot at this stage detect without accountability. Seeds planted in his mind have brought him a false sense of entitlement that tips the scales out of our favor. He walks into a room, and girls run to give him attention. Lots of students want to talk to him. He feels like he's on top of the world. Everyone seems to love him. Davis is listening to the crowd, taking in their praises, and basking in the glamour of popularity. He has forgotten the Psalms.

"Blessed is the man who walks not in the counsel of the wicked, nor stands in the way of sinners, nor sits in the seat of scoffers" (Psalm 1:1)

There's a tremendous spiritual pull here, away from the Lord. But it is subtle and stays just below the surface, undetected by Davis. We are fighting what is to the humans an invisible war.

L

November 4

Littleton,

College is a great battleground. Few Christian students on college campuses wake up one day and consciously turn away from the Lord or reject Christianity. Rather, our enemies slowly turn up the heat until, like a frog in a kettle of hot water, the believer dies a slow and subtle death.

Without a strong connection to Jesus, students can fall into a taxing lifestyle of trying to outperform each other. They devote lots of effort towards looking the best, partying the most, scoring the highest grades, or getting in with the popular crowds. They'll devote enormous energy to meet demanding social expectations in order to be accepted by their peers. It's evil at work in this culture, spiritual warfare so masked and so very ordinary it doesn't get a second look. But these young people can experience point-for-point the list of seducing sins found in Galatians: jealousy, rivalries, dissensions, divisions, envy, etc. Why would our enemies employ a raw, destructive pitch-forked brand of evil when strong, deceptive social currents can keep someone from the green pastures and still waters of God's grace?

Typically when God calls people to the mission field, He gives them a friend and sends them out in twos. Loving the Lord while immersed in student culture requires a one-foot-in, one foot-out-approach–and the foot out is a spiritual community of solid believers committed to doing life together. Does Davis at this point have enough grounding to hear the Shepherd's voice?

Every day, before I leave the war room, I think through all my mentor assignments by name and ask myself if there is anything else I can do to help any of them. When I came to your name today, I thought, *Tell Littleton his persistence is exceptional.* Your relentless pursuit of Davis will help to put him in the best possible position that his heart will allow. All of us on this assignment are fighting for spiritual breakthrough.

Most sincerely,

AM

November 8

Archangel Michael,

Please look closely at this photograph of Davis and his three pledge brothers leaning against a wall at their fraternity party.

Davis is looking at the camera with a casual gaze, almost indifferent to the prepping and posing around him. I see in his expression a sense of resilience, a real promise that he has the potential to walk independently from the culture around him, but I also see a growing danger of too much familiarity and comfort with this world. His indifference could swing either way.

And now consider the scene below, capturing the early part of the evening. Here is my reenactment along with a brief commentary. Notes to follow.

Saturday night, 9:00 p.m.

Davis and three of his new pledge brothers, hanging out in his big brother's room on the second floor of the fraternity house. All of them dressed in button-down Oxford shirts or polos with their hair styled long enough to assure the layered, southern swoop was in full effect. Davis nailed this look in a mere two minutes. The four of them were ready at 9:00 p.m. but in no way considered walking down the main stairs to enter the party until at least 11:00 p.m.. Why should they? A periodic peek out the window revealed a line starting to form. They waited until exactly 11:20 p.m. Perfectly timed to be fashionably late. Lots of hype as the four walked down the stairs and made their appearance. Elizabeth and a group of her girl friends ran and hugged Davis and his friends.

Shouting over the music, Elizabeth said, "A group of us are going to the Bahamas for spring break. We've got a place there. Why don't you come with us?"

"Hey, thanks. But I'm signed up to go on a mission trip to Kenya."

"Oh, no. Well . . . you could do that in the summer, couldn't you?" She smiled and tossed her hair. "Spring break is for having fun!"

The two were interrupted by a widening dance circle that engulfed them and drew them into the crowd. Guys were shot-gunning beers; favorite songs were playing. It was a night of great revelry. Yet it was also a night to fuel the voices telling each of them, "You are the man." How could they not feel that way when surrounded by such a crowd? The attention Davis and his pledge brothers enjoyed continued well into the early morning. Every weekend, it's pretty much the same scenario.

Davis is far from maintaining a one-foot-in, one-foot-out approach. He's in continual spiritual decline, and some days I wonder how much influence I can have on him. But Jesus has reminded me that we have something on our side that our enemies cannot fathom. Davis misses deep conversations. He's surrounded by dialogue always hovering just above the surface. I think the two years of authentic friendships he made in youth group grounded him. For Davis, something will always be missing in his life unless he can get back to relating to people the way he did in high school.

"For all flesh is as grass,
and all the glory of man as the flower of grass.
The grass withereth, and the flower thereof falleth away:
But the word of the Lord endureth for ever."
1 Peter 1:24 (KJV)

The Lord gave me a dream to send him last night, and it played in his unconscious as clearly as a movie scene. Several college students were waiting outside the elevator of a hotel in New York City. When the elevator opened, one of the students pushed the others away and rode it to the top. Exiting and climbing up to the rooftop, he yelled with his hands in the air, "Look at me. Look up here at me! I'm as good as it gets. I'm the best!"

When Davis awoke, he looked up at the ceiling and whispered, "What a dream." He immediately got up and opened the curtains, gazing out the window at the campus. After a few seconds he said, "There's real danger here." I think this dream gave Davis a visual of what an all-in, live-for-yourself lifestyle really looks like.

Archangel Michael, there's a powerful force here urging this way of living, one far deeper than simple social pressure from peers.

L

November 12

Littleton,

Allow me to take you back in history to the year 1646:

A group of men talked and wrote together, dipping a long, black feather into ink and penning their missive on open pages spread across the table. We were there, Littleton. We were in the room, steadying their hands, whispering ideas into their minds and encouraging them always to "Remember the Lord. Remember the Lord."

They were on a mission, those early American men. The first University would inspire all students–the clergy, and in the other professions as well–to view their life vocations as sacred callings. The first code of college statutes of 1646 stated:

Every one shall consider the mayne End of his life and studyes, to know God and Jesus Christ which is Eternall life. John 17.3 (KJV) *

The University would exist for the glory of God and for the common good. However, the cultural currents Davis feels are steadily dragging him away from the Lord. Student culture spurs him to build up his personal brand at all costs. The entire University discourse steers students this way:

- What classes do *you* want to take?
- What major do *you* like best?
- What groups do *you* want to join?
- What are *your* passions?
- How can *you, you, you* capture the most out of life?

---

* Morison, Samuel Eliot. *The Founding of Harvard College*. Cambridge, Massachusetts: Harvard University Press, 1935.

Sin sets in. Prayers dry up. Bibles sit dusty on shelves. A half-hearted effort to stay connected to the Lord can in no way counteract such forceful cultural currents. Students become too busy and too distracted with the electricity of it all.

We need something to jar Davis out of his patterns.

AM

November 15

Archangel Michael,

Elizabeth sent Davis a text message this afternoon about their small group project.

"Hey. Great idea for group project . . . found a Twitter feed to an article 'keeping a country appearance while living in the city.' Link to follow . . . perhaps we need to do field research w/ a shopping spree?!"

Davis's text response:

"Ha, a great way to justify buying more clothes!"

Please provide a background on Elizabeth. I will keep you informed if anything significant progresses.

L

November 16

Littleton,

We ran a quick search. Here are the results:

Name: Elizabeth Anne Hawkins

Relationship to Davis: A new friend in similar Greek-system social circles who is also a colleague of his applying for the business school.

Spiritual biography: Elizabeth believes in the Lord and grew up going to a Methodist church on Sunday mornings with her close-knit family. She is the oldest of two girls. The Hawkins family is dominated primarily by the personality of her father, who owns his own law firm and places a high value on being well connected to his community. He sits on boards for non-profits and business start-ups. When Elizabeth was in high school he told her more than once, "Just remember, you're a Hawkins," a comment meant to remind her to always represent the family well.

One day, in the fall of her Sophomore year of high school, Elizabeth heard a sermon referencing Luke 12:48:

"Everyone to whom much was given, of him much will be required, and from him to whom they entrusted much, they will demand the more."

She underlined the verse in her bulletin. This became a landmark moment for her. She gave canned goods to the needy on special Sundays, and bought hygiene items for struggling families in third-world countries. She volunteered tirelessly with school fundraisers and the student government association.

And she logged a vigorous thirty minutes on the treadmill, five days a week, to stay fit. She did many good things. So, she found her value in these works, in what she did, not in who she was—a child of God, loved and accepted, with an identity that comes from Jesus. Elizabeth never knew the warmth of a close Christian community, nor the joy of approaching her loving heavenly Father and drawing close to Him.

Elizabeth prays on Sunday during Church Worship, but this is as far as her faith goes. The rest of her week is primarily spent approaching her classes with excellence and aggressively completing sorority pledge requirements. To a lesser extent, she enjoys time with her friends. She is attractive and lots of students (guys and girls) like her and would love to spend more time with her. But her drive to perform blocks the chance to get to know anyone really well.

Last night Elizabeth left a dinner conversation in the cafeteria a little early to return to her room and review her grades. Estimating her GPA to be a 3.8, she slammed her pen down and sat back up in her chair. Then she said aloud to her roommate, "Do you think I can ask Professor Maine to do extra credit in Biology?"

Through her father, Elizabeth has already secured an internship on Capitol Hill this upcoming summer. What's interesting is that college in general (and sorority life in particular) is starting to awaken her to invest more time into relationships. Having a big sister, being a part of a pledge class, and going to regular social events encourages this. Her most important relationship, however, remains fairly dry because Jesus is kept at arm's length.

Stay close to them.

AM

November 18

Archangel Michael,

Thanks for the update. Davis asked Elizabeth to his fraternity's upcoming dance. She accepted right away.

This is a semi-formal event, and Davis and four of his pledge brothers are taking their dates to dinner before going to the dance. Post-dance plans are still tentative.

L

November 19

Littleton,

Davis certainly has the clothes for the dance, thanks to the salesman at the men's clothing shop.

Elizabeth isn't what we would call a spiritual encourager, but I'm glad to hear the guys have asked dates to the dance and are taking them to dinner. We've actually seen a wane in dating over recent years; dances are one of the few areas left that help to keep an element of formal dating alive. Otherwise we are seeing a real drop in any situation in which a guy has to initiate effort. Strong cultural currents these days discourage young men from sticking their necks out and being courageous. *Just do nothing*, the world tells them. And if something happens, it happens. That's the mindset.

But the reality is that this forces the young lady to step in and fill the void. First, she must approach him and initiate conversation. Then she has to coordinate a few social events so the two of them can come together (all this in lieu of him asking her on a date). She often must keep putting herself out on the line without a hint of how he feels about her. Time passes. Guess who is the first one to open up and share feelings?

Our enemies have subtlety crafted a cultural trend that runs contrary to the Holy Scripture's reason for marriage, as stated in Ephesians: To be a reflection of Christ and His Church. They've replaced active love with passivity. It runs rampant on college campuses and is reflective of what happened on that fateful day in the Garden.

Adam and Eve were together in the Garden, shining bright
with the love of God. These were innocent years, the best
of times for all of us. King and Queen, the two of them.

Then the Serpent slithered in. Somehow he got his way, tempting Eve to supplant God as the center of her universe. Adam just stood there and let the whole thing happen. He didn't protect her and refused to intervene. He just *stood there.*

Eve was enticed and sinned, taking a bite of that forbidden fruit. She turned to Adam and offered him a bite.

He knew better, but he followed her lead and took it out of her hands anyway. That second dreadful bite.

When all was said and done, God went directly to Adam (not Eve) and asked him why he let it happen. *Adam, you to whom I gave spiritual headship, why did you let this happen?*

You should become keenly aware of how the Genesis pattern reveals itself in the world, and then follow Jesus' lead to reverse the cultural current. Be prepared–young people are easily confused, and neither sex knows how to act. In college, most pairing up happens late in the evening and under the influence of alcohol. For many of them, it feels easier than figuring out how to properly date the opposite sex. But they still have to wake up the next day and face themselves.

I hope this letter is beneficial to you. Remember what I said earlier, Littleton, about a man being hard-wired for respect. A young lady won't respect a man who won't grow up, or one who is lazy rather than active. The princess inside her wants to be pursued.

Few ministers offer sound Biblical guidance in these areas, but there's bound to be someone around campus if you search hard enough. Think about older mentors. Perhaps a college minister or volunteer? A mature upperclassman?

AM

November 21

Archangel Michael,

I decided to remind Davis that it's time for another haircut. A haircut costs only twenty dollars and twenty minutes, and the godly counsel comes free.

I introduced the topic of male leadership in dating by first guiding Robert's gaze toward the television screen during a news flash. Though he couldn't see me, his eyes unconsciously followed my fingertips. I wanted him to see the breaking story about a professional athlete arrested for drunk driving, an athlete who is already under fire for marital infidelity. This started a conversation on marriage, one that I'm pretty confident Robert has had hundreds of times before. And so, because Robert is so good at what he does, the discussion quickly moved to the Ephesians passage on marriage, and the pattern of love between Christ and the Church.

Here is an excerpt from what Robert told him:

"You know, Davis, today's male neglect of leadership in dating and marriage is really just a forgetting of the Lord. Your generation's grown up with the Internet, and some of you think you can hide behind that stuff. But there ain't no shortcuts in life. Intimacy is just something you gotta get comfortable with. And the closer you are to God, the easier it is to open up to people.

"Today when a guy sneaks off in private to a computer to engage in something he shouldn't be doing, he finds it so easy. Just show up at the screen. No vulnerability, no honesty, no intimacy. He can be the king of his imaginary world. And the woman on the screen? She's the object for him to exploit. But no matter what he thinks, the experience becomes a part of him. And it affects more than just him. If he's married—and there are many who are—he puts his relationship with his wife in a terrible position. He loses touch with her. And guess what? He can't really have any real friends, either. Cause he's got a secret. And he's become accustomed to a pattern of secrecy in his relationships."

Robert is exceptional. And he's inspiring to watch. During this exchange he was positioned behind Davis, cutting the back of his hair. And he was leaning in when he spoke. I could tell he feels real purpose in what he's doing. Davis wasn't saying much. So Robert continued, and jumped right into marriage.

"A husband's role in marriage is like the man's role when a couple is dancing. One has to gently lead or the two will trip all over themselves. If done right, what does this look like early on, before marriage? A gentleman finds a lady attractive, and so he pursues her with all that he has. He makes himself vulnerable. He takes her out to dinner. They talk a lot, rather openly. Laugh a lot. He gets to know her in what the Bible says is 'an understanding way.'

"What does she like to do? What makes her laugh? Gives her confidence? Makes her feel safe? What encourages her to stay intimately connected to Jesus, the only one who can truly love her unconditionally? He notices the details. He listens patiently. And as time goes on he gets to know her better and better. Because he's actively pursuing her in the way Christ pursued the Church and 'gave himself up for her,' as it says in Ephesians for the man to do.

"Guess what happens when the man does this. She respects him. Not because of what zip code he lives in, or because of his pedigree, or how much money he has, or what his job is, or anything else. The lady respects the gentleman because he's loved her as Christ has loved the Church. Like dancing, this is one of the most beautiful things in the world when it's done well. It's not easy though—make no mistake about that. It takes a lot of work. It's something you work at every day for the rest of your life, but it produces the greatest of joys.

"If there's a young lady you're interested in, love her like this, Davis. And when you trip and miss a step—because you will; we're all human–repent. When she harms you, forgive. Don't dwell on things, and never keep score. Just keep loving and don't let the Accuser bring you down."

Davis was silent through Robert's entire speech, but his expression showed contemplation. I have high hopes he took in every word, and I will continue to encourage him to develop a relationship with Robert. He needs a mentor.

L

November 23

Archangel Michael,

Davis and Elizabeth enjoyed the dance. Socially, Elizabeth handled herself well, staying with Davis for most of the night but also mixing with others when they became separated in the crowd. A pivotal moment occurred between them later that night.

As the evening faded, Davis and Elizabeth walked onto the balcony of the country club overlooking the golf course. They leaned over the railing side-by-side, looking out into the stars and every so often at each other as they laughed about the evening and talked more openly about college. Elizabeth pulled her hair over her far shoulder and leaned closer. Davis was surprisingly transparent. He brought up the Lord and his struggle to find spiritual community.

"I love it here, but it's still kind of lonely."

"How so?"

"I don't have any strong Christian friends like I did in high school. I miss 'em. You know what I mean?"

Elizabeth hesitated and looked down. She deflected the question away from herself, "Don't you . . . go to The Edge?"

"Sometimes. But it's probably not going to be my faith community. I need to look somewhere else."

"Well, everything happens for a reason," she blurted, and then quickly changed the subject to talk about her upcoming internship in D.C. on Capitol Hill.

Davis replied, politely, "Sounds awesome." He then called out to a couple of his fraternity pledge brothers who approached the balcony with their dates, and the six of them talked as a group until the night faded and it was time to take their dates home.

Davis seemed reflective for the rest of the weekend. On the Monday, following the dance, Elizabeth raised her hand in class. When called on she began to give a better answer than the student in front of her. At the time Davis was looking down at his notebook, so I helped to turn his gaze upward so he could focus on Elizabeth and hear her response.

The way she phrased her answer revealed it was meant as a slight affront to the other student–a way for Elizabeth to gain points with the professor. "I actually . . . think it's more accurate to call this a luxury goods market. The term upscale is too vague."

I'm unsure how much this helped, but I'm hoping it at least gave Davis more perspective on Elizabeth.

L

November 26

Littleton,

I now see more clearly why God said, "Littleton is extremely clever and has been tailor-made for this environment."

Seeing the Lord's providence clearer and clearer.

AM

November 28

Archangel Michael,

Far from Davis's room, on the opposite side of his dorm floor, there's a student from Texas with a military haircut who wears mostly jeans and cowboy boots. I've noticed him walk down the hall several times, with a weathered black Bible with the name "Cody" printed on the cover.

Compared to a lot of the other students, he doesn't say much. But he seems to be watching everyone closely and taking in conversations, especially in the dining hall. He's been eating at Davis's table lately. I've been watching this guy.

If you have time, please keep your eyes on their dorm hall tomorrow at approximately 7:00 p.m. After dinner, Davis plans on going with Cody to an event at Cody's church. It's the church's annual Harvest Evangelism Conference. Be ready to watch the full evening's events.

L

November 29

Littleton,

Powerful! Really powerful to have Davis go with Cody to the Harvest Evangelism event! I ran intelligence on Cody. Here's what I have:

Name: Cody Jackson

Relationship to Davis: Neighbors in the same dorm floor and a newer friend through conversations in the cafeteria. The two have had a couple of late night talks.

Spiritual biography: Cody is from South Texas and the boots he wears are handmade—his grandfather bought them for him last year for his birthday. His granddad was an oil and gas landman who drove a black Chevy pickup truck. Everyday at exactly 1:00 p.m. he would pull his truck over to the side of the road and fix himself a whiskey and Coke. Cody's dad followed in his father's footsteps in the oil and gas business, black Chevy truck, whiskey and all, but he started doing more deal-making than land work. During Cody's first summer working for his father, his dad shared his secret for business success.

"When I consider funding a new oil team, I already know the guys are good at what they do. I'm listening to see if they can admit failure or if they always have an excuse. And do they love their work, or are they merely seeking a large, quick payoff? Are they plainspoken, or are they trying to impress me? Those are the qualities I'm looking for."

Cody learned to observe and read people at a young age. During his freshman year of high school, a Young Life leader reached out and befriended him. Cody's father had just hit a string of oil finds in a row, and all of a sudden their family had a private jet and two ranches stocked with cattle, four wheelers, and jeeps.

But the newfound wealth added unexpected tensions and pressures and created a lot of family strife. His dad worked around the clock and stopped caring about Cody's sporting events, or coming home for the family's evening meals.

While all of this was going on, this Young Life leader took Cody aside at a retreat and shared the Gospel with him. Cody's been running hard with Jesus ever since. He transfers the stubbornness he inherited from his grandfather and father, and the tenderness he learned from his mother, to God and his friends. You notice he woke early on Saturday morning to study, and then drove away from campus without any books? His former Young Life leader had called unexpectedly on Friday night and said that he would be in town on Saturday and could swing by campus for an hour around midday. Cody woke up early, finished his essay, and then drove an hour and a half (each way) to buy beef jerky from the best place in the state. The two of them used to eat jerky during his high school years when conversations went well into the night. Cody associates beef jerky with this Young Life leader and the way he used to help Cody sort through the confusion of a conversion and a newfound life.

Cody is wise and discerning for his age, but being primarily an observer of others he struggles with the large social demands of being at college. He's hesitated to dive deeply into community because large groups overwhelm him. However, find him one-on-one or in a small group and he flourishes. Cody has watched Davis's roommate, Andrew, rather closely this year, and he sees through the pretense. He's also impressed with the way Davis handles himself. Cody likes Davis a ton, and he's determined to help him grow closer to Jesus. Christians like Cody and Robert are invaluable to us in our assignments. Remember in Biblical times when we watched Saul relentlessly attack and try to kill David before he became King? The Accuser thought he had David cornered, isolated without a friend in the world. And then Saul's son, Jonathan, rose up for David, about as loyal a friend as you could get. Boom. David turned the corner.

By the way, we have all been following the Harvest Evangelism Conference with real interest. To have 50,000 people in a stadium listening to a sermon, and to have 1,000 churches across the country broadcasting it live, makes it the largest evangelism event of the year. Many of the social commentators and a fair amount of today's ministers don't expect America to turn back the secular tide. They think America is now post-Christian and destined to take the secular trajectory of other countries. Some are reading the polls of shrinking church membership and the loss of faith as signs of biblical prophecy from the book of Revelation.

But they always try to do this–predict the future–though Jesus clearly told his disciples, "It is not for you to know times or seasons that the Father has fixed by his own authority." If you look back through the ages, the doomsayers seem to pull out their megaphones at most major pivotal events: during times of great war or famine, at the turn of each new millennium, or after any significant natural flood, disaster, or catastrophe.

To be clear, Christianity is taking a significant hit in America, and unlike in many other parts of the world it has been in decline. The social impact this is having on people and families is devastating. But America has been in far worse spiritual shape than this. Back in the 1730s, fewer than ten percent of the colonists believed in the Lord. Then preachers like George Whitfield and Jonathan Edwards started preaching the Word with great boldness. The First Great Awakening swept through the country like a brush fire fanned from above. People started to pray. And pray they did. By the end of the First Great Awakening, the Spirit had swept through the hearts of men in America with such overwhelming force that most of the population committed to Christ and joined a local church. Move the clock forward to the 1820s and the Second Great Awakening pushed back the skeptics once again and caused another tremendous spike in converts.

Littleton, we see the Holy Spirit sweeping through this country again today, refreshing a few dying churches and planting many new ones. These churches are growing like wildfire, reaching the lost, healing the sick, strengthening the downcast. They're doing it by preaching the pure unadulterated Gospel. We notice the arts taking root in these communities, and powerful worship with an emphasis on healing the inner life. Keep this in mind as you look to make connections for Davis on campus.

Could America be on the brink of another Great Revival, or will the erosion of Christianity continue? Time will tell. We angels don't even know. But we certainly are going to do as much as we can to aid spiritual revival wherever the Lord assigns us.

By the way, did you notice tears in Davis's eyes when he saw people walking to the stage to become Christ followers during the Harvest Evangelism Conference? The Holy Spirit touched him deep inside. I've added several new angels to our team to surround both Davis and Cody.

AM

December 1

Archangel Michael,

Praise the Lord! Davis's friendship with Cody continues to deepen. We arranged for Davis to catch a last-minute flight so he could meet Cody and seven of his Texas friends at his family's ranch. I'm with them now and they're having a blast. They're mudding, and Cody let Davis drive a few of the guys in one of the open jeeps. You should've seen him dodging tree limbs and flooring it over large puddles of water. All the guys returned caked with mud all the way up to their faces.

They spent the better part of this afternoon shooting (this *is* Texas, after all). Lots of guns, and lots of steaks to grill afterwards, along with several tightly-rolled high-grade cigars. Cody's friends are genuine Christians–full of salt and light, as Jesus would say–much like Davis's youth group and an excellent contrast to the cultural Christianity they've been running into in their dorm hall.

The weekend did a lot for him. Cody's friends put Davis at ease, and he seemed to intrinsically understand he didn't have to impress them or to prove his worth. To be around a group of guys like this doing "guy stuff" was for Davis the "green pastures, still waters" of Psalm 23.

L

December 2

Littleton,

Way to go!

Christians like Cody and his Texas friends constitute a minority on most of the college campuses around the country. The majority of college freshman would probably say that God has little to no impact on their lives. Here are the stories of three college students, who recently shared their experiences. It will give you a better idea of the sort of brokenness we're dealing with in this campaign, and why Davis could have such a difficult time keeping up a vibrant faith. The article shines a spotlight on three different people:

Carl–A second year student talking to himself out loud after a recent phone call with his father: "I can't stand him anymore. So what if he made a lot of money? I never saw him. Now he's trying to force me to follow in his footsteps. No way. Don't care what he says. He can't control me anymore. And no one–I mean no one–will tell me what to do ever again."

Ryan–A capable college minister, replying via text to a request to join a student ministry team here on Davis's campus: "Thanks for the offer, but I've had enough. I'm tired of having three, four, five coffees a day with students because I can't afford the meals. Raising support has put a tremendous strain on my family. The businessman I met with last week decided to build yet another resort home. So he couldn't recommit his support pledge for next year. I think it's time for me to go into business instead of ministry. Unsure what. It really doesn't matter. Our eleven-year-old car doesn't have much life left. My wife deserves so much more."

Piper–A student who lies on the table, limp and listless, inside the nurse's office. Part of her conversation with the nurse: "Oh dear. How long have you had an eating disorder?"

Piper shrugged, her expression numb. "Four years, I guess."

"Am I the first one you've told?" The nurse put her hand on Piper's forehead, but she flinched away.

"Yes."

"Well, I am so glad you did." This time, when the nurse reached out, Piper didn't react. "We'll get you better."

Tears sprang to Piper's eyes. "I'm just . . . tired of living like this," she whispered.

And so the quiet battle rages in this campaign, in the midst of tests and homework, football games, marching bands, dorm food, student theater performances, dances, keg parties and late night hook ups, video games, campus ministry, and pizza. Most of the larger population has no idea that the battle for the next generation is being fought in everyday circumstances right under their noses. It is our job, Littleton, to engage the battle where the humans don't see it.

Keep up the good fight!

AM

December 7

Archangel Michael,

Last night wasn't fun. Davis received a text message from one of the fraternity brothers:

"All pledges be at the house at 10:00 p.m. No exceptions."

I followed Davis over there, and the closer we got to the house the darker it grew. Several fallen angels blocked the front door as I approached. I tried to fight my way through them, but I couldn't get in. Davis walked through the doors to the sound of loud, thrashing music. For the next two hours I fought one demon after another, struggling to break in. No luck. But then I saw an opening on the rear of the house and slipped through into the foyer.

All I could hear was screaming and yelling. Then all of a sudden it stopped. The pledges walked out the door in a single file line. Davis looked troubled–offended might be a better word. I walked home with him, all the while popping a message into his mind. *Christ is King. He's the King.*

I just kept repeating this same message over and over again. He walked into his dorm room and went straight to bed. I don't know what happened in there tonight, but I hope I can make something good out of it.

L

December 8

Littleton,

Take heart. We're in these campaigns for a reason–they are spiritually dark places. And that always means the demons will have a lot of resources to draw from.

There is a principle in war strategy, however, that may be helpful to you. When facing an opposing army that is larger and stronger than you are it's usually best to not attack them head-on. That would be a battle of attrition. The odds are they'll run over you.

You should instead aim to outmaneuver them. Approach the war from a different angle. Attack them in an unexpected way; use your speed and agility. You're looking for weakness in their armor. You're in this specific place, fighting this specific case for a reason. *Littleton is extremely clever and has been tailor made for this environment.*

Think laterally. We are firmly and resolutely fixing our eyes on Jesus and believing in spiritual breakthrough.

AM

December 10

Archangel Michael,

Thank you. I'll keep my eyes open.

Today I arranged schedules so that Davis and Cody could have lunch. I thought Davis might open up to Cody about last night. As they sat down to eat together, Cody asked, "How's it going, Davis?"

"Pledging, man. It's not fun."

Cody sat back and a knowing look came into his eyes. I could tell he knew exactly what Davis was going through, so I nudged him to encourage Davis. "I know, man. Hazing. You're not supposed to talk about it. But it's real."

Cody shook his head. "And degrading."

"Yeah. And I hear we're one of the lightest hazers of the big houses," Davis said.

"I've got a friend at the University of Texas who's a lot like you—trying to make an impact for Christ in the Greek system. He said he's sick of the hazing and that he won't do it to pledges when he becomes a brother."

"Amen to that. But sometimes I think this whole thing is stupid. Why do we do all of this?" Davis said, playing with his food and not looking up.

"Look, I can tell you're having a hard time and I won't force you to tell me the details if you don't want to. But I think for you it's probably worth sticking through," Cody said.

Davis sat up straight and put his fork down. "Why do you say that?"

"Davis, you're cut out for leadership. I know we haven't known each other for very long, but I can see it in the way you walk and how you carry yourself. It's with you wherever you go."

"Really? Thanks, I guess. But what does that mean?"

"Greeks hold the most influence on this campus, and it's an

influence that carries beyond the college years. I would advise you to stay where you are . . . and be in it, but not of it." Cody laughed. "Sorry to sound clichéd, but it's true."

Davis started picking at his food again. "I guess I should probably pray about it."

"Yeah. Of course! Pray about it, man. That probably should have been the first thing I told you to do." Cody gave a self-deprecating smile. "But it seems to me you need to stick to your guns. You could have a lot of influence here. That's my two cents, at least. Take it for what it's worth."

After the two parted ways, Davis stopped to sit on a picnic bench. He was reflective, I could see it in his eyes. Then something hit him. His face lit up, and he grabbed his phone and starting writing a group text message to all of his pledge brothers:

"Guys—I'm wondering if you want to commit to never hazing the new pledges once we're initiated. We don't like it done to us, so we won't do it. Thoughts?"

He received a mixed reaction to his text, though a lot of the messages were positive. You should've seen how curious and excited he was to read those texts as they came in. I touched his shoulder to strengthen him. There's definitely something going on that goes deeper than freshman hazing. Something hit a nerve in him and caused his leadership instincts to kick in. Take note of this follow-up text exchange Davis had with one of his pledge brothers:

"You're taking this too seriously. All they did was yell and stuff."

"Yeah, but it still wasn't right."

"Maybe not. But they're not like . . . like hitting us or making us drink."

"True. But they're not really making us closer brothers, either."

"I don't know man. Maybe it's the religious thing with you. Or that Cody guy. But you're getting too serious. Lighten up."

"I just want everyone to think it through. If it's not a good thing, then why do it?"

Archangel Michael, this showed me Davis has strong convictions and he's not afraid to share them with his peers.

I love this guy!

L

December 12

Archangel Michael,

Yesterday I watched Davis in the library working on a research paper. He created two piles of books. The first was a collection of biographies, letters and commentaries on President George Washington. The second had the same but pertained to Robert E. Lee. Davis then spent the next forty-five minutes whipping through texts, turning pages quickly, underlining passages and writing down notes with firm strokes of his pencil, and then writing comments on his legal pad.

I couldn't really make out what he was doing because the comments seemed so unrelated. Oh, I could read a phrase here about "gaining a strategic advantage" or a comment there about "troop responses," but most of his notes were written in the margins rather than in outline form. And then, ever so often, he would circle a phrase and map it to another one.

Davis then put these books down, paced back and forth, and walked over to the journal section. He saw an article entitled, "Effective Decision Making: Gaining Perspective from Four Military Generals" and picked it up. I couldn't describe to you how wide his eyes lit up as he read the article.

After reading it, Davis returned to his desk with his legal pad and pile of paper. He flipped through the pages of his notes several times. And then he paused, and I saw his eyes look down and to the right. He turned to his laptop and wrote this sentence:

"Love and Respect: the hallmarks of legitimate authority"

I can only say after observing his interactions with others that leadership must run through his veins. And if that's the case, it's something I can work with. It might be the angle you talked about. And it also helps me to see more clearly why Andrew's methods bother him so much.

_L_

December 13

Littleton,

Keep digging; we love what you're finding.

Here's an interesting statement from the intelligence report we just received:

"Davis Lewis Chandler has been reading the biographies of American presidents since he was twelve. He wrote his final senior year thesis paper on George Washington's principles for living. He titled the paper: "President Washington: Civility that Shaped the American Spirit."

Littleton, it's been my experience that when a person has something unique in his background, something that person really enjoys, the Lord wants to use those influences for His glory. They become part of the "good works" that a person is called to do.

"For by grace you have been saved through faith. And this is not your own doing; it is a gift of God, not a result of works, so that no one may boast. For we are his workmanship, created in Christ Jesus for good works, which God prepared beforehand, that we should walk in them." (Ephesians 2:8–10)

As you circle the campus, perhaps hover over spheres relating to history and government and find out what opportunities might be on the horizon for Davis. Try to find something interesting. And challenging.

AM

December 19

Archangel Michael,

That's great news. Finding leadership opportunities is definitely on my radar. But it will have to be next semester because finals have ended and Davis is now on Christmas Break.

Here's what happened the first night he returned home from college. Davis and his family had supper at one of their favorite seafood restaurants, a reunion meal lasting two hours. Lots of warmth and laughter. And by the way, I noticed that when Mr. Chandler asked questions, he seemed more focused on the big things: grades and intellectual development, friends and Fraternity Rush, and church attendance.

Davis's mother and Ansley, on the other hand, loved listening to his college stories–who he is friends with, what they do, and in particular any girls he mentions. I've noticed Davis doesn't talk intimately and openly about the Lord in front of his parents, though they seem to assume God is an active part of his life. They're happy with how Davis's first semester has turned out, particularly since he scored a 3.8 GPA and seems to be getting along well socially, too.

After dinner, Davis caught up with his former youth group at Jonathan's house, which has billiards, dartboards, and a movie room. I can see it was probably a popular place for the church youth group during high school ministry years. This visit did wonders for Davis. They laughed easily. They encouraged and built each other up, even in humor, and they intermixed comments about the Lord while talking about dining hall food and football games. It was as if the group had never separated to different colleges. Later in the evening, as the refrigerator ran out of ice, I encouraged Jonathan to ask Davis to go get ice with him so they'd have an opportunity to talk alone.

As they drove off together, Jonathan told Davis of the close friendships he had made at his university with a group of Christian guys.

"Two of them live on my floor and three others are in the dorm next door. These guys are so solid. We pray together often and they spur me on to Jesus."

I hope it doesn't escape Davis's notice that, when Jonathan talks about his college experiences, he talks about the Lord quite often. God is an active part of his friendship experiences and is invited into the various parts of his life. He talks as openly about Jesus as he does about the Atlanta Braves or country music.

Jonathan continued. "I've also started working out at the gym with this guy named Lake. We're getting pretty close. He was a quarterback in high school, a popular guy. Lake's parents forced him to go to a Christian college because it would 'keep him out of trouble.' But Lake doesn't know the Lord and he feels a little out of place here. We get the chance to talk a lot at the gym. He's started opening up to me about girls and friends and what's hard about being there."

Jonathan nodded and smiled at Davis. "I know Jesus brought us together, you know what I mean? It's just one of those relationships."

Davis turned to him and said, "I wish I had your confidence in how God's leading me. You're closer to Him than I am. That's . . . kind of tough for me to admit, honestly."

"Hey, it takes a lot to admit that. Feel like telling me more?" Jonathan replied.

The two of them shared a moment of silence. Then Davis continued, "There's a void in my life. We've talked about it. I know a bunch of people, but hardly any of them really well. Listening to you makes me realize I really miss our youth group."

Davis shrugged and scratched his chin before speaking again. "I still don't have a faith community. I have a good friend named Cody and a few others who are Christians, but not a ministry I can call home. Until now, I couldn't see how much this has affected me."

"I bet that's lonely, brother. Let's pray. Let's pray right now."

"Let's do it. Pray for me, bro."

Jonathan bowed his head and placed his hand on Davis's shoulder. "Jesus. Sweet Jesus. Bring my brother Davis a community of believers–real brothers and sisters in Christ. Prepare this group for him now, Lord. And prepare him to be ready for them when he returns from Christmas break. Bless our spring break mission to Africa, Jesus. May we all grow close to you. We ask all this in your name. Amen."

When Davis went home that night he prayed on his knees, echoing Jonathan's prayer for the Lord to provide a campus ministry group for him. And he made a firm resolve to actively look for one come January.

I couldn't be happier. It was amazing to me how grounded and at ease Davis appeared after reconnecting with Jonathan. I see now why you keep pushing me toward this end. Friendship is everything!

L

January 6

Archangel Michael,

Christmas break is drawing to a close and it's done wonders for Davis. There's one more conversation you should know about. Davis met with Jason Allison, his former youth minister, at Starbucks. Here's part of the conversation that stood out to me as Jason listened to Davis's stories.

"Remember last year? In Bible study? How we prayed every Wednesday. You always wanted guidance for your first year of college."

"Oh, yeah," Davis said. "Yeah, I remember that."

Jason continued, "You talked a lot about joining a fraternity and being a witness for Christ in that environment. I said two things then, and I feel like I should repeat them now. First, don't blindly accept and recite any preambles, pledges, oaths, or anything that conflicts with the spirit of Jesus. Second, if you feel called to live in that world you'd better be anchored in a Christian community. A fraternity can't be your community. You need to be different than the world. A shining light. And a witness for their sake."

"Thanks, Jason. I needed to hear that. It's been tough with my roommate and The Edge. No excuses, though."

"There's got to be another ministry out there. The Lord's not going to leave you dry."

"Yep," Davis said, smiling. "You're totally right."

Davis needed the break and these guys came through for him. He's returning back to campus strong in the Lord again.

L

January 12

Dear Littleton,

We're clashing with fallen angels who have had a stronghold on this campus for years. The fighting has been intense. Last night we split their troops to the east and west, forcing them to fight on two fronts. To the east we were for the first time able to capture a favorable artillery position. To the west I sent a new team to attack their strongest and most seasoned Legion. Our guys engaged them head-on in a devastating barrage, driving the line until the center started to give way. They recovered and held their ground, and we had to retreat. But Littleton, we're starting to drive them back!

Fortify Davis's dependence on God. And if you get the chance to put him into a leadership position, take it.

AM

January 17

Archangel Michael,

Yesterday I spent some time at the student center listening in on conversations and looking for leadership opportunities. I overheard a mature-sounding older student–a junior named Hampton–talking to a girl named Caroline about running for student body president.

What Intel do you have on Hampton?

L

January 18

Littleton,

You hit solid gold! Here's Hampton's dossier:

Name: Hampton James Post

Relationship to Davis: A fellow high school alumni who is two years older than Davis, though the two did play on the same lacrosse team. Hampton and Davis have yet to run into each other on campus.

Spiritual Biography: Hampton is sharp both intellectually and spiritually, and he's one of those guys who has been from an early age. During the senior awards ceremony at high school, Hampton laughed as he walked up to the stage to receive his framed certificate that read "Most likely to make senior management by the age of thirty." A *Summa Cum Laude* with a double major in Business and History, on the inside of his wallet he carries a white card with a black-scripted font that says, "Everything for His Glory." He's highly respected on campus and leads a Bible study for freshman guys.

Hampton and his girlfriend, Caroline, are on leadership with a Christian student ministry called TRU, which is led by a very capable college minister named Will Harton. Hampton met Caroline during freshmen orientation his first week of school, and the two have known each other socially and through the student ministry ever since. Last year during a retreat, they were asked to co-lead a team of freshmen.

Hampton noticed the inner and outer beauty of Caroline the second day of camp when he saw her hug a crying freshmen girl as the two were sitting on a rock overlooking a valley. That evening he asked her to dinner for the Saturday after camp ended, and the two have been dating and growing close to each other ever since. With some guidance from the college minister Will, and his wife Anne, but mostly from their own efforts in seeking the Lord, their relationship is on a solid foundation. Many of their friends flock to both of them for Christian counsel and dating guidance. As a couple, they radiate with joy and clearly love spending time together. Caroline is becoming one of Hampton's wisest counselors, and Hampton's shoulder is Caroline's favorite resting spot to lay her head.

AM

January 23

Littleton,

News came in from Jesus himself. He wants you to deliver an angelic message to Hampton. You are to work Davis into Hampton's campaign team for student body president. And since Davis has lately been praying rather fervently for the Lord's guidance, we're adding several new angels to cover Davis, Hampton, and Caroline.

I look forward to hearing how you deliver this message.

AM

January 24

Archangel Michael,

When I found out Hampton planned on taking his campaign team out for barbecue, and then to return to his room for a strategy session, I stayed with them through the evening. Dinner was interesting. Lots of storytelling, and no campaign talk whatsoever. It seemed to me that Hampton wanted the guys to bond and to get to know each other. And he never talked about himself at all. Fascinating.

The team then returned to his room for a strategy session. As they mulled over campaign ideas, I noticed Hampton's senior high school yearbook on his bookshelf. A few minutes later, Hampton said, "Guys, we need to add an additional person to help secure the freshman vote. Let's think about who might be good for that."

I immediately helped one of the students fix his eyes on Hampton's yearbook. When this student pulled the yearbook down from the shelf to flip through it, I had the book open to the large photo of their lacrosse team kneeling on the field with sticks in hand.

Hampton looked down at the photo, recognized Davis in it, and said, "Davis, of course! I wonder if he would be interested."

L

January 25

Littleton,
    Clever move. Nice touch.

AM

January 26

Archangel Michael,

Once Hampton found out Davis lived in Clifton dorm he walked over to room #206 and knocked on the door.

Andrew answered the door. "Oh, hey. What's up?"

"Is Davis here?"

"No, he's probably at class."

"Would you tell him that Hampton Post stopped by? Here, give him my telephone number." Hampton wrote down his phone number and gave it to Andrew.

"I know who you are. You're one of the leaders of TRU. I'm one of the leaders of The Edge."

"Oh, that's great. Y'all have a great worship team. What's your name, man?"

"Oh, thanks . . . uh . . . Andrew. Andrew Mason." He reached to shake Hampton's hand and asked, "How do you know Davis?"

"We went to high school together. Tell him I'd like to catch up with him."

When the conversation ended and the door closed, Andrew went into Davis's room and looked up Hampton in the yearbook. "A Junior. That's interesting," he whispered. "I wonder what he wants with Davis." He wrote a short note attached to Hampton's name and number and left it on Davis's desk

When Davis returned, he saw Hampton's number and sent him a text message right away. After the two decided to meet at the Student Center at 3:00 p.m. tomorrow, Davis sent one more question:

"Anything particular?"

"Yeah. I'm running for student body president, and I want to talk to you about the elections."

Davis read the text and smiled. He immediately answered:

"Sounds good. I'll be there!"

Andrew then walked into the open doorway of Davis's room and asked, "Did you see Hampton's number?"

"Yeah, thanks. I just sent him a message."

"I didn't know you two knew each other. I know him, too. I saw him last week. We're both on a committee for our Day of Prayer event."

Andrew paused, his head slightly lifted back. I think he may have wanted Davis to join in and say something like, 'No way, you know him too!' But he didn't get that.

"What did he want?" Andrew then asked.

"He . . . probably just wants to catch up since we haven't seen each other since I got here."

It's sad to see Davis and Andrew live without much joy or trust between them. I suspect that if Davis had another roommate he would have shared about the election and about how the two of them played lacrosse together. I'll keep working on this relationship. But for now, I'm grateful the message was delivered and I will make sure Davis gets there on time.

L

January 27

Archangel Michael,

Davis woke up in the middle of the night and lay in bed for a few minutes, trying to go back to sleep. He walked into the kitchen and ate a bowl of cereal and then returned to his room. It took him awhile to get back to sleep. He didn't pray to God, and he didn't say anything. He just lay there for a while with his eyes open, and it seemed as if he was thinking about something. Eventually he closed his eyes and lay on his side. I touched his forehead so that he would sleep. But he woke up two hours later to the sound of a loud delivery truck that stopped on the street in front of his dorm.

Davis got up and into the shower. I heard him then say, "What's wrong with the hot water?" and saw him turning the shower knob back and forth. At this point I suspected something was up.

A text message from Elizabeth came across his phone:

"Professor Sanders replied to our outline. Wants us to redo the case review. He needs it by Friday."

When Davis turned on his computer he couldn't find the file that he had been working on. So he had to start over again. At 2:50 p.m., Davis realized he was running late and started jogging across campus. His phone fell out of his pocket and a corner of the screen cracked.

Our enemies couldn't keep Davis from making the meeting, but they certainly wanted him weary and frustrated for it. I could tell he was hungry, and before Davis arrived at the student center, I saw a group of girls setting up for the Blood Drive. They were unpacking bags of Rice Krispie treats and apples that they were about to give out. So, as Davis walked in I prompted one of the girls to hand him some (even though their table wasn't set up yet). Then I reminded him of his friend Jonathan to pick up his spirits.

A tired Davis walked into the Student Center at 3:00 p.m.

"Davis!" Hampton smiled as the two caught eyes and walked towards each other. They shook hands and then gave each other a pat on the back with their free hand. Not much small talk as Davis jumped right in:

"Good to see you Hampton! Running for president, huh?"

"Yes. It's something I've been thinking about for a while. Our campaign's off to a solid start."

"Sounds exciting. What made you want to run?"

"Well, there's a lot to say. Toward the end of last year, our student body president pulled me aside and talked to me about running. After prayer and some wise counsel, I started to feel the call."

Just then a demon rushed in through the doorway and headed straight for them. I intercepted him by leaping into his pathway and fought him back. We wrestled for a while. He was screaming and making hideous noises and reaching his hand out trying to touch them. I thought to myself, *don't let anything ruin this meeting*, and I kicked out his leg and saw a chance to lock him up. He fought pretty hard, but I pinned him down with his face against the floor. He was scratching and groaning and making noises, but I realized that if I listened closely, I could still hear faint sounds from their conversation:

"We need someone to join our team who can work on the freshman vote. You'd be great. I remember how much everyone loved you on lacrosse, even when you were only a sophomore. So what do you think?"

"Totally! Let's do it!"

The demon stopped fighting.

"Awesome!" Hampton and Davis slapped hands. "Our campaign team meets next week and I'll send you an invite. You can meet everyone then."

"I look forward to it!"

We're in, and I'm pumped. I see now how important it is for Jesus that Davis nurtures his leadership calling.

L

January 28

Littleton,

A vicious storm blew in last night. The worst I've seen in a long time. Reports came back of screeching yells from legions of demons who attacked our guys. We were wounded pretty badly.

Darkness is coming across all of our assignments on campus.

Our scouts tell us the demons see what you're doing. They plan to fight at all costs to keep Davis from going on the mission trip.

Dig in and hold your ground.

AM

February 7

Archangel Michael,

They're coming back strong. I fought off several demons in Davis's marketing class, but one of them flew right into Professor Sanders at the end of class. Seconds later Sanders said, "I've been looking at our schedule, and we're running behind. I'm in the process of revising our syllabus, but I wanted everyone to know ahead of time that we will be having a major exam the day after spring break. Sorry about that. I'll have study sheets out as soon as I can get to them."

Class ended and many students were murmuring under their breath about how unfair this was. As Elizabeth and Davis walked out of class, she said to him, "That's frustrating."

"I know, I can't believe it," Davis said. He then started walking toward an outdoor table in the Quad. "That's two exams and a paper due the day after spring break. I'm supposed to be in Kenya."

Elizabeth then noticed Andrew walking by about fifty feet away. "Speaking of mission trips, she said, Andrew keeps talking to us about his. He's, like, obsessed with it. He almost makes me feel guilty for not going on one."

"I know," Davis said.

"But what's wrong with going on spring break with your friends? Doesn't God want us to have close friends?"

"Oh, sure he does."

"It's not like we're going to get into trouble. My parents will even be there for a few days."

"Andrew's really . . . caught up with things right now. The Edge and . . . being on leadership," Davis said.

"I think mission trips are great. And I love helping people. But I don't really see the point of short-term missions. You won't be able to get to know someone from another country who you only see for a week. It's our first year of college. We need friendships."

"Yeah, I see what you mean. If I go to Kenya it would be great to serve. But it would only be for the week," Davis said, nodding his head.

"So you're at least *thinking* about the Bahamas?"

"Yeah, I'm thinking about it."

"Great! We'd love to have you."

Davis sighed and said, "I'm going to wait and see what the study sheet looks like. If both of my exams call for short-term cramming, then I probably won't be able to go away for a week. I'll need a few days to study."

Davis's eyes then lit up and he added, "And oh, did I tell you that a guy from my high school invited me to join his campaign to run for student body president? As head of the freshman vote, I could use those days to plan and strategize, too."

"That's so cool! You're going to be, like, running this place. Everyone's going to know who you are."

Davis grinned.

They're skilled manipulators, Archangel Michael. Elizabeth likes Davis, so she was trying to get him to go on the trip and to spend time at her family's place. Of course she had no idea that three fallen angels were constantly bombarding her thoughts during their talk. They were steadily cheapening Davis's image of the Kenya trip with her comments about short-term missions. Listening to Elizabeth, I can tell she's never been on a short-term mission trip, because if she had then she'd know you get really close to the people you go on the trip with and serve alongside. But Davis's friend Jonathan is hundreds of miles away, too far away to give Davis another immediate perspective on this conversation.

How can we avoid these tactics? Or at the very least, minimize their damage?

L

February 9

Littleton,

You're feeling the sting of Davis not being connected to a community and in a small group Bible study. If he had a group of guys he regularly met with, he would be getting support in all these areas. He would've been airing out his frustrations with Andrew, and they would have been praying for him. He'd have instant accountability and people praying with him about the campaign. They'd help him keep his heart in the right place because Christ would be right in the midst of their circle, guiding their paths

"For where two or three are gathered in my name, there am I among them." (Matthew 18:20)

A lion always attacks the lone prey.

Keep telling me anything that relates to Elizabeth, Andrew, and missions.

AM

February 10

Archangel Michael,

Davis really enjoyed the campaign team, and I can see this assignment is giving him a new-found sense of purpose. Here's a short exchange.

"Team, I'd like you to meet Davis Chandler, a really cool and talented guy I knew from high school. We actually knew each other from lacrosse. Davis played on the varsity team as a sophomore. He's going to lead our efforts at gaining the freshmen vote."

Davis then received a warm welcome from the team and answered a few questions about his involvement on campus, the Sigma's, and the dorm he lives in.

"I'm really psyched about Davis joining our team," Hampton said. "He's really well-liked. Everyone in high school loved him."

"Hey, thanks. I can't wait to help. I'll map out the different social circles I'm in—high school connections, greek system, major, people I've met from The Edge ministry—and come up with a game plan so I can show it to y'all."

"I didn't know you were involved in The Edge," Hampton said.

"I was early on. Not as much anymore but I still know some of the people," Davis said with his head slightly down.

"Okay, let's talk about that sometime." Hampton replied, and then turned the conversation toward the next topic of developing his campaign platform.

I could see that Davis was in his element. His eyes were wide open as the group began to discuss leadership and strategy. As soon as they got out of the meeting he called home and told his parents.

"Hey, Dad!"

"Davis! How are you? Wait, let me get your mother." Mrs. Chandler also picked up the phone and the three of them had a short conversation.

"Guess what? Remember Hampton Post from our lacrosse team my sophomore year?"

"Phillip and Beth's son, sure," his mother replied. "Great family."

"He's running for student body president and he asked me to join his campaign."

"Oh, Davis, that's great news! Leadership experience is something you can't get enough of!" Mr. Chandler said.

"I'm sure Hampton runs around with a good crowd," Mrs. Chandler added.

"Thanks, I know. It's a great opportunity."

"I'm sure it is, but just make sure you keep up your grades," Mr. Chandler said.

"I know, I know," Davis said. "I will. I'm excited to be working with these guys."

Little does Davis know that this comment is probably the key to his freshmen year. If a friendship forms with Hampton I'm sure he'll bring Davis by TRU. And just like that, community forms again. The Lord seems to be working on multiple levels here–Christian community, leadership, and a calling that will give Davis something to do and keep him from too many social distractions.

Wow, I'm seeing lots of promise! Need to get back on the battle of the Kenya mission trip, so Davis can sit at Pastor Pete's feet.

L

February 14

Archangel Michael,

Not so great news, I'm afraid. When Davis and Elizabeth received Professor Sander's study guide, Davis read it over for a minute and said to her, "It's a lot of material. More than I thought."

"Yeah, and mostly memorizing stuff. I'm definitely going to need the time on the beach to study." Elizabeth shot Davis a quick glance.

As the two of them walked out of class together, Davis said, "I don't know how I'm going to pull all of this off. If my other test ends up being like this one I won't be able to go to Kenya."

Elizabeth asked, "Are you certified for Scuba diving?"

"No. I've never had a reason to be."

"Well, our friend Chris is a licensed instructor. He's going to help a group of my friends get started on certification this weekend. It'll only take a few hours."

"Wow, that's great!" Davis said.

"Do you want to join us? We're meeting tomorrow at two, and we have room for one more. I just thought, you know, it would be a great thing for you to have even if you don't come with us."

"Yeah, that's a good idea. I'll come by and take a look. Thanks. Just text me the details," he said.

When Davis met up with Elizabeth's friends, they all talked with anticipation about the trip. No one pushed him, but they made it seem like paradise. Here's Elizabeth approaching her friend Caitlin, who was sitting right next to Davis.

"Check out these pictures. The reef is absolutely gorgeous." Elizabeth leaned over far enough so that Davis could also see her phone.

"That's beautiful. I can't wait," Caitlin said.

"It really is," Elizabeth said with a smile, looking at both Caitlin and Davis. "You can see it from our deck. We have so much fun just looking out at the water."

Davis stared at her pictures for a long time.

Needless to say, we continue to lose ground. I don't know how to stop this.

L

February 18

Archangel Michael,

They're bringing Andrew into the picture again. It's starting to get ugly. Here's another conversation between Elizabeth and Davis while they were walking home from class.

"Andrew sent my roommate and me a support letter about the mission trip he's going on. I'm sure you got one, too." Elizabeth frowned.

"Yeah, but I haven't read it."

"Listen to this," Elizabeth said, pulling the letter out and opening it. "'God's called us to tell the Good News. Our generation needs to rise up.' It's like, I get it, but Andrew seems so self-promoting."

"Ha!" Davis raised his eyebrows and covered his laugh with a cough. "Why do you think so?"

"Because he says 'our' and 'us' like he's the guy who's going to fix everybody's problems. Also, have you noticed how he's always trying to invite girls from the three most popular sororities to go? I wonder why *that* is." Elizabeth smirked.

"You're definitely on to something!" Davis laughed more openly.

The worst part of this exchange came later that night. Davis received a letter from Jonathan about the mission trip to Kenya, and it had the same line in it: "God's called us to tell the Good News." He read this line out loud, so he must have remembered it from Andrew's letter. He put the letter aside, laying it on a stack of papers on his desk.

I think our enemies have almost turned Davis off to the Kenya trip. Piling on homework was bad enough. And now all of Elizabeth's comments about spring break being a time for friends, along with both of their criticisms of Andrew's sincerity, seem to have drained some of his enthusiasm. When he thinks about Kenya, he may automatically think about Andrew and his mission trip. It's a repeat of what happened in the fall, when one bad experience at The Edge was enough to keep him from pursuing other student ministries.

What am I to do?

L

February 19

Littleton,

We're in these campaigns for a reason. They are spiritually dark places. Once evil gets entrenched, it's difficult to overthrow.

You should see what's happening in our sex-trafficking campaign. We make small gains–a few volunteers, a little money donated to our cause, a church that's willing to offer some care to victims trying to get out of slavery-but as soon as we start softening an abused girl's heart, she struggles with accepting genuine love. Our enemies haunt her with fear and prey on her vulnerabilities. It's a bitter struggle right to the point of liberation.

Just keep doing whatever you can to get him to Kenya. Make it priority number one and wait for an opening.

AM

February 21

Archangel Michael,

On Saturday, Davis lay on his bed trying to take a short nap. Andrew was in the living area with the door ajar, talking on the phone to a student named James. He probably thought Davis was sleeping.

"So, how big is his lake house?" Andrew asked. After a short pause, he said, "Wow. Forty? That's a lot of people." Another pause. Then, "Yeah, I know it can fit all of the first years. But . . . hey, let's . . . keep it exclusively for the ministry team. We need to have a weekend to ourselves. And that would be a lot of fun."

Davis rolled his eyes and shook his head. He then whispered, "Not surprised." He got up and started walking out of his room.

Andrew hung up the phone. When he saw Davis, he asked, "What's up?"

"I'm going for a run. How about you?"

"I'm leading a prayer meeting with our freshmen from The Edge who are going on our mission trip for spring break." He paused. "Mission trips are so important. These students will really grow from this."

"Yeah, I'm sure," Davis said without much vigor.

"Looks like I'll be leading some devotionals while we're there."

"That's great," Davis said. But I got the sense he wasn't overly enthused.

"You can join our prayer meeting if you want. Maybe you'll need the support."

"Maybe," Davis said, and then he left the room.

I could tell from Davis's expression that he had no interest. At this point, any effort Andrew makes to minister to Davis meets nothing but skepticism. But even worse, the personal conflict between the two keeps damaging Davis's impression of mission trips in general.

It's a pretty sophisticated manipulation; I haven't seen our enemies this focused since I started here. And they've definitely been effective. Later that day, Davis received a text from Jonathan that read,

"Mission trip is looking good. I just sent some devotionals to you by email."

Davis read the text, but he never looked at the email. It's still unopened in his inbox.

L

February 23

Archangel Michael,

I can't win this battle. The demons are so subtle in their deception, and Davis can't see it. He needs to be a hundred percent all-in, with missionary zeal, in order to take the academic hit for going. But they're steadily stripping any purpose he felt. When Elizabeth talks about Andrew, she's insightful, and Davis recognizes it. And she and her friends are physically attractive and well-spoken, and they look like they're ready to take off for a coastal weekend. I'm guessing the exact background, taste, and style that Davis has been accustomed to being around. They're comfortable together, and Davis is adopting her view of short-term missions.

Any effort on Andrew's part brings nothing but skepticism. The slow erosion of Davis's zeal has been so real. I've watched it clear as day.

Archangel Michael, it's becoming overwhelming. What am I to do? They're in every detail."

L

February 25

Littleton,
 Death couldn't stop Him.
 The grave couldn't hold Him.

AM

February 28

Archangel Michael,

Thanks for that!

I haven't found an opening yet. It's been hard to even slow down what is going on. Cody's slammed with work, and Davis is too distracted to make any significant effort to see him. I did have Davis book another haircut, but here's how the conversation went as he walked up to Robert.

"How've you been, Davis? What have you been up to?"

"Oh, nothing." After the two shook hands, Davis said, "Sorry I'm a little late. I just got finished talking to my mom."

"How's your family doing?" Robert asked.

"Good." Davis stepped into the barber's chair. "Looks like I'll see them for a day before heading out on spring break."

"That's good. Where are you going?"

"Still deciding, but probably to the Bahamas with a group of my friends. My friend's family has a place there."

"Will their parents be there?"

"Yeah, for part of the time at least."

"That's good. Avoid those spring break trips that can get you into trouble."

"Yep," Davis replied. And I got the sense that he thinks he made a wise choice, because he raised his chin ever so slightly.

The two changed subjects, and spring break never came up again.

L

March 3

Archangel Michael,

Davis received his study guide for the second exam and immediately started texting Jonathan.

"I'm really sorry, but I've got two exams and a paper due the day after spring break. I think it's best for me to pull out. Let's do another mission trip over the summer."

Jonathan's reply was almost immediate.

"You got your shots done, right? And you already have a passport?"

"Yeah. But I'm slammed and I feel so behind. Haven't even been keeping up with your devotionals. Even if I could go I don't feel ready to go. Physically or spiritually."

"It's not really about being ready as much as it is about just showing up. The Lord will use you."

"I know He can. But I think I just have too much going on."

Davis waited a minute and then added:

"I can go with some friends to Elizabeth's place in the Bahamas for a few days. Not a party trip. I can just show up and not plan anything. Then I'll have three free days at home to see the fam and get my work done."

"Hmmm . . . Man, we'll really miss you. If you change your mind, there's still a place for you with us. You gotta know that."

"I do. Thanks! Can't wait to be back at home again this summer."

And so the conversation ended. I was terribly disappointed that Davis backed out. But I have already started thinking about how we can turn this around for good. Perhaps I can encourage him to use his last few days at home with his family to be thinking about the campaign. We can use that time to build up his faith and nurture his calling.

L

March 7

Archangel Michael,

Davis drove home fully packed with clothes for the Bahamas and all of the academic books he needed. He arrived in time for dinner, and Ansley greeted him with the warmest of hugs, screaming "Davis!" as he entered the front door. His parents followed.

"It's so good to see you!" Mrs. Chandler said as she walked up to give him a hug.

"And I hear we are going to have a few extra days with you?" asked Mr. Chandler.

"Yeah, that's right. I'll only be gone for a few days. My friends are picking me up tomorrow at 10:00 a.m. Our flight leaves at 2:00 p.m."

His reunion with family was everything they hoped it would be. Davis spent a lot of time showing them some of the pictures that he'd taken of a few of his recent social events and explaining the stories behind the photos. When Mr. and Mrs. Chandler went to bed, Davis stayed up and talked with Ansley for a while. Here's one of their exchanges.

"How's the youth group?" Davis asked.

"It's been great. But a little awkward with Will. He's been texting a lot. And he took me to Chick-fil-A the other day and paid for both of us."

"Definitely sounds like he's interested in you."

"But I only like him as a friend."

"Sure, Ansley. Maybe next time he asks you to go somewhere, ask him if it's okay if you bring Kaitlyn along also? Or one of your other girlfriends?"

"That's funny. I was thinking about doing that."

"And hey, don't forget, it's a compliment to have a guy interested in you. Let him down easy. You can pay your own way from now on if he offers. And if he keeps pursuing you can just tell him you really appreciate him as a friend. But not for dating."

"I know. I will," Ansley said, smiling. "I will." Then after exhaling a deeper breath, she said, "I really miss you, Davis."

"I miss you, too."

It's good to see them reconnect. The two are thoughtful with one another, and Ansley really brings out the tender side of Davis. It's the same with Mrs. Chandler–Davis's mom and sister are more warm and open with their feelings, and it seems to ground him. Just an observation. Davis ended their conversation by telling Ansley he needed to get ready for bed, but he looked forward to having more time to hang around when he got back.

In the morning he awoke early and finished packing. The doorbell rang at 9:45 a.m., a little earlier than he expected, but Davis had just finished packing. Davis opened the door to find Jonathan and Jason.

"The van's ready. We're on our way to Kenya. Come with us," Jason said.

'I . . . can't. I've just finished packing for the Bahamas."

"That's all right, man. You can go there some other time," Jonathan said.

"My friends are coming. And I . . . still have all this work, and you guys are gone all week."

"We know. But you're smart; you'll figure it out. Come on, we gotta have you!" Jason said.

"Just bring your Bahamian clothes to Kenya. Who cares?" Jonathan said.

"Well I . . . feel really rushed here. Ummm . . . let me think for a minute." Davis left them in the open door and paced into his parent's living room, running his hands through his hair.

"Your parents won't mind your going with us!" Jonathan said, calling through the still-open door.

"I . . . I . . ." Davis sighed and shook his head.

I figured this was my last chance, so I flew back and forth through his body touching his heart, giving off enough warmth to stir emotion.

"Alright, I'll go!" Davis said. He told his parents and then quickly sent a text message to Elizabeth that he'd changed his mind.

Against all odds, we are now on a plane headed for Kenya!

L

March 8

Archangel Michael,

It's a powerful experience. Davis is being transformed from the inside out. Here are a few of his journal entries:

Day 1

I'll never forget flying in and seeing those zebras roaming the grasslands. It's so beautiful here! Even though I was exhausted from the flight I didn't close my eyes for one second on the drive from the airport. The grasses stretch flat to the horizon in every direction and there are enormous, spreading, flat-topped trees all over. I'll have to look up what they're called when I get home, but for right now, I just want to soak it all in. I saw one giraffe as we drove, but no animals other than that and the zebras. I'm already glad I picked this over the Bahamas. I can tell it's going to be the trip of a lifetime.

Day 2

Still getting used to the poverty in this land. I've never seen anything like this before. People aren't just hungry here, they're gaunt . . . stretched. Their eyes reflect a hopeless resolve to go on existing as long as they are able before they lie down and give up.

I'll admit to a degree of shock on my end that left me virtually speechless as we went door-to-door through the Rift Valley village today. At every stop our team leader Doug would knock on the door and kindly address whoever answered it—usually a woman or a girl. Before leaving each house, we always asked, 'What can we pray for you about?' The response was unanimous from house to house: 'Rain. Please pray for it to rain. We cannot grow our food without rain.'

We must have prayed for rain fifty times today. And around midday—it's still so incredible, I can hardly think about it without getting emotional—we saw clouds gathering over the redstone mountains that ring the valley. I've never experienced God's presence like that! I still can't believe he really answered our prayers so quickly. It hadn't rained in the Rift Valley in four months! By late afternoon, as we climbed into the van to drive out of the Rift Valley, raindrops were starting to splatter against us. By the time we got back to our dorms, rain was coming down in a soft, steady sheet.

My God, I've taken so much for granted in my life. I can turn on a faucet and have water whenever I need it. I've heard of droughts before, obviously, but never before today have I seen the effects of one. Praise God for the rain today. Praise God for answered prayer!

Day 5

We began our ministry in the slums of Kibera today, and I'm still reeling. I thought I was prepared to enter that place. I was wrong. Millions of people living in abject poverty. Miles and miles of corrugated, rusty metal shacks. Human waste flowing in narrow rivers through the streets. And orphans . . . orphans everywhere. We pulled up at the charity school in our van and were immediately surrounded by a hundred smiling faces, reaching hands, and choruses of 'How are you? How are you? How are you?'

I'm ashamed to write this down, but I froze. For a moment my horror of the poverty overwhelmed my reasons for being there, and I wanted nothing more than to stay in the van. Gabe, a guy on my team, reached over and squeezed my shoulder when I didn't move to get out with the rest of them. 'Hey man, you all right?' he asked. He kind of snapped me out of it, and I was able to get out, greet the kids, meet the pastor who runs the school, and go on with the rest of the day.

But I admit, I don't remember much else. The suffering I saw today among children who shouldn't have to suffer . . . I can't even express what I'm feeling! When we got back in the van to leave the slums tonight, I just let it all out. And I wasn't the only one. Nobody talked on the drive back to our hostel, and I don't think there was a dry eye in the van. I can only earnestly pray that God helps me to overcome my emotions and the weakness of my flesh so I can better serve those children tomorrow.

Day 8

Last day today. We spent it in Kibera with the kids, whom I've grown to love more than I would have thought possible in such a short time. I'm so thankful God gave me the strength to overcome my initial fear and shock so I could have a truly rich time with them. We taught Bible classes today, led the kids in some praise songs, distributed the books and toys we brought from home. It was tough to say goodbye to the kids. Several of them clung to my arms as we were leaving and begged me to take them with me. It was one of the hardest things I've ever had to do–to look into those hopeful faces and say that I was sorry, but I couldn't. These kids truly have virtually nothing to look forward to in this life. I hope I can get dad to help them out. And I pray that many of them came to genuinely know Jesus this week so that they can have hope for eternity. It breaks my heart.

Then the evening came and I was shattered. I sat back and listened to Pastor Peter's amazing sermon. I wish I could remember it word-for-word because I would transcribe the whole thing here!

I'll take it from here. Here's a transcript of the last evening, the most pivotal moment for Davis. Feel the energy in the Kenyan minister's voice as he preached with great joy following the Lord's healing the broken arm of one of his church members. Davis sat in the front row of the orphanage during the sermon, and his eyes were fixed on the minister every second.

Scripture Reading:

"Now he was casting out a demon that was mute. When the demon had gone out, the mute man spoke, and the people marveled. But some *of them said, 'He casts out demons by Beelzebul, the prince of demons,' while others, to test him, kept seeking from him a sign from heaven. But he, knowing their thoughts, said to them, 'Every kingdom divided against itself is laid waste, and a divided household falls. And if Satan also is divided against himself, how will his kingdom stand? For you say that I cast out demons by Beelzebul. And if I cast out demons by Beelzebul, by whom do your sons cast them out? Therefore they will be your judges. But if it is by the finger of God that I cast out demons, then the kingdom of God has come upon you. When a strong man, fully armed, guards his own palace, his goods are safe; but when one stronger than he attacks him and overcomes him, he takes away his armor in which he trusted and divides his spoil. Whoever is not with me is against me, and whoever does not gather with me scatters.'" (Luke 11:14–23)*

Sermon excerpt:

"What we saw today was a healing. A healing from the Lord. The power of the Lord. It came from the Power of the Lord. The POWER of the Lord. The power of THE LORD! CHRIST OUR KING!

"In this text, Jesus is talking about being the strong older brother.

"People saw a mute man unable to speak. He saw EVIL.

"Evil overpowering the weak. The innocent. The one who cannot defend. And He came in His power and *took it out*."

Everyone in the room got to their feet and cheered, and it took Davis and his friends only a moment of hesitation before they joined in. These Americans aren't used to such lively participation in a sermon! As the pastor continued, the people remained on their feet, and some of them stomped a rhythm to his words, making the rest of the message almost an act of corporate worship.

"Anytime we have power–any kind of power–we have spiritual power. Spiritual power to let the Lord come in and attack EVIL. He wants to attack the Evil with his POWER."

There was a pause as the people shouted affirmations and clapped their hands.

"America . . . America does not understand this message. Too selfish . . . Her people are too focused on themselves.

"CHRIST has given her POWER. Money and influence over the whole world. She needs to use the Power. American Christians need to let Jesus use their POWER."

He continued preaching for some time, but I could tell Davis was already broken. He wept out loud and covered his face. And he didn't stop weeping through the rest of the sermon.

And then he prayed. "I'm so sorry, Jesus. I had no idea how far I'd drifted from you. So sorry. I've been living for myself. I can't wait to get back to campus. Lead me, God. Lead me."

Archangel Michael, we now have a heart set ablaze.

L

March 18

Dear Archangel Michael,

Davis is experiencing extreme culture shock after returning from such dire poverty. Students all around him are having fun, but he's not engaging and he seems depressed. He called his dad a few days after he got home. Here's part of their conversation.

"I don't know. I just don't feel the same after coming home."

"What don't you feel the same about?"

Davis sighed. "About life. Classes. Campus activities. Everything, really. It all seems so superficial now."

"I'm sure everything will go back to normal after a while. Get caught up on sleep and back into the swing of things and you'll feel better soon. You can't feed every starving orphan in Africa."

"No, but I wanted to ask you about that."

"Oh?"

"I know you like a good tax write off . . ."

"I think I know where this is going!"

"Well, how about it? Living Waters Church and Orphanage, where we did our ministry work in Nairobi, would be a great organization to support. And they could really use the help, Dad. If you could have seen those poor kids you wouldn't even hesitate."

"Send me the info and I'll consider what to do about it, okay?"

"Okay."

"And in the meantime, get to work on that campaign! I'd love to see you elected to office there on campus."

"Sure thing, Dad."

But when Davis hung up the phone, he put his head in his hands and cried. I touched his heart to encourage him and he prayed to God for strength. Then he pulled up his Kenya photos on his laptop and whispered prayers for each of the orphans he saw in them—by name for those he could remember.

I think he was unprepared for the emotional toll that returning from the mission trip has been. In Davis I see a desire to do something to stave off the depression; hence his request for his dad to support the church in Kenya. But he's also relying on the Lord and selfless prayer to strengthen him. I'm encouraged. I'm sure you will be too.

Regards,

L

March 20

Dear Archangel Michael,

Our enemies prey on Davis's thoughts night and day. They don't want him to take on leadership in the campaign. Here's a conversation from yesterday between Davis and Elizabeth.

"How's the presidential campaign?" Elizabeth asked.

"It hasn't started yet. We're meeting next week."

"That's exciting. You'll be really popular. And your next three years will be set," Elizabeth said as she smiled.

"Yeah, maybe. But after Kenya, I've lost my zeal for that sort of thing."

"What do you mean?"

"It's just . . . . Why does it matter if we win student body president?"

"Because you're the best ticket, right?"

"I think so. From what I know. But I really want to make an impact for Christ here."

Elizabeth paused for a second. And then she said, "You know, you can . . . do a Bible study and help out that way." She paused. "But Davis, you're never going to get a chance like this again. You're crazy if you don't do it. Think of what it will do for your resume and connections."

As soon as the conversation ended, six demons approached Davis carrying messages. I fought them off as best I could, but three of them broke through and slipped thoughts into his mind. I did hear Davis whisper afterwards, "Why is this campaign so important?" Judging by his facial expressions and general attitude, the demons were effective. He's not smiling very much, and I can tell he's feeling down. While walking across campus, he whispered, "God, I'm not going to get caught up in being cool. I'm not going to climb the ladder."

I wish I could get Davis to understand that he can glorify God in the way he desires by serving on student government, but he's too

aware of his frailties right now. And that's what the demons are prey-
ing on–they're trying to convince him that he's only helping with the
campaign because he wants to be cool. As we did many years ago
with William Wilberforce, we must convince him that he can be both
a public servant and a Christ follower. And that in his case, the two do
go together.

But how do I do that?

L

March 21

Dear Littleton,

I've seen this many times before. Evil often comes in strongest when they've had to concede ground. They know that once Davis is plugged into community and following Jesus' lead in serving, they won't have much influence on him. As you astutely noted, they'll try to guilt him with "Two Spheres" thinking: The church and the world are two separate places. The world is a bad place, avoid it at all costs. Stay in the church.

Remind Davis of the words of Jesus:

"You are the light of the world. A city set on a hill cannot be hidden. Nor do people light a lamp and put it under a basket, but on a stand, and it gives light to all in the house. In the same way, let your light shine before others, so that they may see your good works and give glory to your Father who is in heaven."(Matthew 5:14-16)

The battleground is in Davis's mind. Don't let them distort the truth.

AM

March 23

Archangel Michael,

It's happening just as you said. Davis talked to his parents yesterday and here's a conversation he had with his father.

"How's the campaign coming?"

"We haven't met yet," Davis said, "but I'm still not totally sure I'm going to do it."

"Why not? You were so excited about it."

"I'm just . . . rethinking what's important," Davis said, seeming to be at a loss for words.

"Your Kenya experience?"

"Yeah, I'm trying to really live for the Lord. I feel like I . . . should do something for Christ. Maybe be more involved in ministry."

"It's great to be involved in ministry," his father said. "But the world works a certain way, Davis. Chances like these are hard to turn down, and you've got to think of your future, too."

Davis hung up and went to his knees. "Father, I want to serve you and have influence for Christ. Everyone's trying to convince me to just go back to doing the same things I was doing before the mission trip. I'm not going to do it."

Davis is pretty resolved to not let anyone's advice influence him. He seems to think he's turning from God if he takes on secular leadership, and so far the two people who have advised him to stay the student government path have used secular arguments to try to convince him. In this manner they don't realize it, but they're actually pushing him farther away from walking that path . . . and farther away from God's will. Davis is interpreting the open campaign door as being the wide and easy rather than the narrow and hard. Our enemies have worked a master manipulation in this.

L

March 26

Littleton,

Jesus wants Hampton and Davis to be together. He sent us some valuable information that's not in our enemy's playbook . . . access to Davis's inner thoughts. It's a snapshot that shows Davis's thinking right before a demon delivers a negative message, and then it shows how the message leads his mind astray and sends him in a different direction. Here are three examples that occurred yesterday.

March 25, 1:15 p.m.

I better get started on my paper. Class is cancelled, so I have a few hours. Perfect. [**Message enters: Why does this paper matter? Who am I to write a paper on leadership?**] *I've never done anything that great. I lived for myself last semester. Why should I be involved in leading other students? Somebody a lot better than me should do that.*

3:10 p.m.

There is something awesome about the spirit of these military generals. I love it. Makes me kind of want to get involved in this campaign. It'd be cool. Maybe the Lord could use this. [**Message enters: I'd be going into the campaign and the debate for my own glory.**] *Yeah. Like everybody says, I'd be doing it to be the big guy on campus. To build up my resume. I'd better tell Hampton to forget it.*

3:25 p.m.

Keep thinking about the sermon I heard in Kenya. Wonder how God could have an impact on our campus. How would he do it? A lot would have to change. [**Message enters: I need to do something Christian. Start a Bible study or something like that.**] *Yeah, I think the elections are more about me feeling important than really helping anybody. Let's be honest. I'm not that great of a Christian. I've got to get involved in ministry.*

Littleton, these messages are effective because Davis hasn't learned that the Spirit within him enables him to claim authority over them. As you can see, when a subversive thought comes into his mind, Davis not only accepts it but he dwells on it.

I'm sure you can see that the messages they are implanting into him have already been reinforced through prior conversations with Elizabeth, his father, and others. You need to work vigorously to reverse the pattern of his thinking.

> *"And be not conformed to this world: but be ye transformed by the renewing of your mind, that ye may prove what is that good, and acceptable, and perfect, will of God." (Romans 12:2, KJV)*

Being transformed in the mind means resisting discouragement just as much as temptations. Help him to think about Christ, not himself. And encourage him to pray and to ask for guidance, rather than rationalizing his decision and trying to solve it with intellect.

AM

March 27

Archangel Michael,

I decided it was time for another haircut. Here's the most important part of Davis' conversation with Robert.

"How you doing? Good to see you again."

"Oh, I'm good. But I'm having culture shock after the mission trip."

"Makes sense," said Robert.

"Yeah, it was really powerful. God is so good. After seeing how He worked over there I'm wanting to have more of an impact for Christ here."

"That's good."

"I'm not going to get distracted anymore. Before I left, I was fired up about taking on leadership in a student government campaign. But now it all seems so unimportant. And I'm not sure I'd be doing it for the right reasons."

Robert's ears perked up. I saw him look away from Davis and then back at him as if he were thinking. Then he said, "Hmmm . . . Davis, what's wrong with a Christian taking on leadership?"

"Oh, nothing. It's just that I feel like I need to do something for Jesus. I think I'm going to back out."

"Maybe you should give the campaign a chance. I cut a lot of hair and I just don't hear young guys mention the word 'leadership' that often anymore. It's a shame. If you're cut out for it then God might want you there. I'll be praying for you. You do what the Lord wants. Let me know how it goes."

I'm hoping this conversation prompts Davis to talk to Hampton.

L

March 28

Archangel Michael,

Jesus approached me directly! He had me send the same message to Davis four times today: **Talk to Cody about the elections.** Seems like after the fourth one it finally settled in. Davis stopped by Cody's dorm room last night. Here's the important part of the conversation.

"I'm going to talk to Hampton and tell him how I feel."

"You mean, tell him you don't want to serve in the campaign?"

"Yeah, I think so."

"I think that's a bad idea."

"Maybe. But it's how I feel and it's my decision," Davis said.

"Look, I'm not trying to tell you what to do. But I just feel like I need to say something. Hear me out."

"Sure, go ahead."

"You know, my dad donates to political campaigns in Texas. And he gives a lot of money. So, we usually get invited to some private dinners with the members."

"Yeah, I would imagine so."

"And I've been going to these things for a while now."

"Go on. Say what you've got to say," Davis said, sounding somewhat eager.

"Sometimes I like these guys, and sometimes I don't. But the ones I like, I really like."

I sensed that Cody really had Davis's attention and was about to make his point. So I nudged him to look down at his sweet tea and stir it. This pause was enough to pull Davis deeper into the conversation.

Cody continued, "Davis, early last semester I saw the conflict going on between you and Andrew before you did. I was impressed with the way you handled it."

"Thanks."

"And I watched you pretty closely during Fraternity Rush to see if you were going to join the Chi house. And you didn't. You resisted a lot of social pressure. And I said to myself, 'This guy's pretty strong.'"

Cody gave a slight pause, and then leaned his head toward Davis and said, "When you did that, I thought about these guys that my dad funds . . . the good ones, the ones I like . . . and I thought to myself–this is what they were like in college."

This conversation definitely had an impact. Davis thanked Cody and went back to his dorm room. He lay on his bed again and opened his Bible. I had him turn to this verse in the book of Esther.

"And who knows whether you have not come to the kingdom for such a time as this?" (Esther 4:14)

It seemed to me like the Holy Spirit took over and touched Davis's heart. Davis underlined that passage and took a few deep breaths. He sat and stared at the verse. Then he reached over to his phone and sent this message to Hampton:

"I need to talk to you about the campaign whenever you're free."

L

March 29

Archangel Michael,

Hampton and Davis met for lunch. Here it is.

"So good to see you again," Hampton said with a smile.

"Thanks, you too."

"How are you liking it here?"

"I like it. But I want to live with more purpose. I want to have an impact for Christ."

"That's great!"

"Hampton, I just better tell you. I'm not sure working on the campaign is my thing."

"Hey, that's okay. Your call. So what do you think your 'thing' is?"

"Don't know. But I just got back from a mission trip to Kenya. It was really powerful, and the Lord spoke to me. He wants me to influence this campus. Not sure how yet but I'm going to try to do it."

"Wow!"

"The minister preached a sermon about taking leadership for Christ wherever you are."

Hampton smiled. "Sounds like a wise guy. What was your takeaway from that?"

"God's shown me I have influence with the freshmen here."

"I'm sure you do; that's part of why I asked you to run with me. But what are you thinking?"

"Like I said, I don't know. But I'm not gonna live for myself anymore. I'm all in for Jesus."

"Davis, that's exactly why I'm running for student body president."

"Really?"

"Yeah, and it's not something I planned to do either. I'd been serving on the ethics committee in student government. One day Jefferson, our current president, came up to me and said, 'Hampton, I've been thinking about who should replace me next year. And I think it should be you.'"

"It's interesting that they came to you. That's a good sign. That's happened a lot in history."

"What do you mean?"

"I've been reading the biographies of our presidents since I was twelve years old. Remember Mr. Huff? I used to talk to him after class."

"Mr. Huff!" Hampton laughed and slapped his knee. "American History. I loved that guy!"

"Me too."

Hampton then pulled out his wallet and told Davis, "During my senior year, after having several conversations with my youth leader and Mr. Huff, I made this card and I've kept it in my wallet ever since."

Davis looked down at the card. It read *"All things for his glory."*

"Most of my involvement on campus has been with student government and the student ministry TRU."

"I really need a student ministry," Davis said. "I need to get that part of my life straightened out if I'm going to do this campaign and do it right."

"Do you want to go with me on Tuesday night?"

"Sure, that would be great!"

Hampton's cell phone buzzed, and he looked down at it. "Shoot. I'm sorry, Davis. I've got to run. Can you meet up tonight? I want to tell you about my vision for leadership. That might help you decide if you want to get involved."

So it ended well. I'm throwing all my effort into making sure the enemy doesn't block the meeting.

L

March 30

Archangel Michael,

Davis went back to his room. Before he opened his Bible he prayed on his knees, "God, I need wisdom. Guide me." Then he opened his Bible and started flipping to the Proverbs. He landed on Proverbs 16.

> *"The plans of the heart belong to man,*
> *but the answer of the tongue is from the Lord.*
> *All the ways of a man are pure in his own eyes,*
> *but the LORD weighs the spirit.*
> *Commit your work to the LORD,*
> *and your plans will be established.*
> *(Proverbs 16:1-3)*

Davis read these first three verses and then prayed, "Father, tell me about Hampton. Are you bringing us together? Do you want me to be a part of his campaign? Does it matter to you if we win? Search my heart, Father. Will I get swayed or be turned astray? Be clear in our meeting tonight. If I feel peace, I'll do it. If not, I won't. In Jesus name."

Later that night, Hampton picked up Davis and drove both of them away from campus to a barbecue place in town. Here's how the conversation went.

"When I think about leadership I think about Jesus," Hampton said. "First, his words that the greatest among you is the one who serves. I think this is the hallmark of a Christian leader. And service means laying your life down for another."

Davis didn't say anything.

"I know politics can get rough. I expect that to happen. People aren't going to always agree with you. Some will be jealous and hate you. You've got to have your identity in Christ alone and no one else."

Davis tapped his fingers on the table, and had a thoughtful expression on his face. "How do you plan to deal with these tensions when conflict hits and you're feeling pressure?" he asked.

"A couple of ways. First, Jesus said, 'I lay my life down for my sheep. No one takes it from me, but I lay it down on my own.' Those words, to me, say keep Christ as your center and stay rooted. A Christian leader is a servant but he isn't a doormat."

After a pause Davis said, "Go on."

"We need to address conflict directly and not let it fester. But the attitude and the spirit of how we approach things is the key. Speak the truth in love. And if we're wrong, admit our mistakes and ask for forgiveness right away. No one of us is perfect. And I think people respond well to an honest person trying to do what's right."

"I would agree with that," Davis said.

Hampton leaned forward, earnest. "I believe with all my heart that this matters to the Lord. He's called to me to do this so it's important to him. But I also know that being active in the world, not shying away from it, is the way of Jesus. He lived it. We're meant to imitate him and to be lights to the world. A light has to shine where people can see it. Wherever the Lord gives us influence, he wants us to use it to draw others closer to Him."

"Hampton, you just described the sermon I heard in Kenya." Davis stopped tapping his fingers on the table. His eyes were shining as if with unshed tears. "One more question. How do you plan on mentioning your faith during the campaign?"

"When it comes up, I plan to just be honest and talk naturally about it, as I would anything else. And the principles of the campaign–the platform we build–will be on solid Biblical principles. That's the first thing the team and I will work on. We're aiming to create the best environment for students to thrive and for God to bless our campus."

"I love it, Hampton. And I've seen it many times before and thought about this a lot as I've read the biographies of our presidents. Okay. I'm in. Just tell me where you need me."

"Awesome! I'm pumped!" Hampton reached across the table and shook Davis's hand. "And I want to hear what you know from history," he said before releasing him. "Your background is extremely valuable."

He's going to do great.

I can't wait!

L

March 31

Littleton,

Angels and demons collide in a bitter fight that continues to escalate. Here is a series of updates that came to me from one of our troop leaders.

March 27: We fought our first major battle and it ended in a bloody stalemate. There's hardly a minute we are not in the saddle.

March 28: We faced relentless attacks from a new legion of fallen angels.

March 29: Their numbers increased as they captured significant positions on campus.

March 30: We fought on well into the night trying not to cede too much ground.

Today, however, a hopeful report came from within our lines. During what seemed like an endless series of attacks, the Holy Spirit blew a strong and forceful wind that swept across the battlefield. Trees swayed to the piercing sound. The wind turned into a tornado that skipped over our troops and headed straight for our enemies, who dropped their swords in horror, retreating in great numbers. And we, an inferior number, chased them far into the night with piercing yells they will never forget. Around the campfire that evening our angels sang well into the night. Our commanding angel posted several pictures of college students from your campus. The last one was an enlarged picture of Davis on his knees, weeping during the Kenyan sermon. When the angels saw this picture they cheered for him.

Moments later, intelligence rushed in from our scouts. Seventy-five new angels are being added to your campus right away. Two vibrant churches decided to increase resources toward college ministries and will be hiring additional staff. A sophomore who has struggled with guilt and shame for years turned to Jesus for the first time. A freshman who lives directly above Davis made peace with his father. Two broken, borderline abusive relationships were mended. A high school senior quarterback from Birmingham–a strong believer active with Fellowship of Christian Athletes–signed a letter of intent to attend next year, and several of his closest friends have agreed to follow his lead. A science professor who is a strong believer has accepted a tenured position beginning in the fall. Two student ministries have increased resources to a point where they can reach nearly double their group of existing students. The gospel slowly, quietly began to spread through the second floor of the all-girls dorm, Penton Hall. And fifty fallen angels assigned to Davis's circles were cast out into the abyss.

It was a beautiful wind, Littleton.

AM

April 2

Archangel Michael,

You should have seen Davis this morning!

One of our angels noticed that the minister at the church where Davis attends would be preaching on the last part of the Sermon on the Mount, so I immediately rallied twelve angels, and we flew to the Church at 10:30 a.m., hovering at the ceiling.

Davis walked alone up the sidewalk, which proceeds up the hill to the church sanctuary. He was well rested, spiritually hungry, and kind to a few people he recognized along the way. He then took a seat by himself.

We heard beautiful worship music before the scripture text was read from the pulpit:

> "You have heard that it was said, 'You shall love your neighbor and hate your enemy.' But I say to you, Love your enemies and pray for those who persecute you, so that you may be sons of your Father who is in heaven. For he makes his sun rise on the evil and on the good, and sends rain on the just and on the unjust. For if you love those who love you, what reward do you have? Do not even the tax collectors do the same? And if you greet only your brothers, what more are you doing than others? Do not even the Gentiles do the same? You therefore must be perfect, as your heavenly Father is perfect." (Matthew 5:43–48)

At this time, we helped Davis look up toward the window at the top of the wall to notice a beam of light shining in from the outside. With a contemplative look, Davis took out his pen and drew a solid rectangular box around the following verses:

"But I say to you, Love your enemies and pray for those who persecute you, so that you may be sons of your Father who is in heaven. For he makes his sun rise on the evil and on the good, and sends rain on the just and on the unjust."

Davis then opened his bulletin and wrote a few notes. And then he started to pray. We were circling above him as he wrote, and we swooped down to strengthen him as he whispered the following prayer:

"Jesus, you know how I feel. I can't stand the guy. You know I did nothing to provoke him. You know how hard it's been for me this year. And you know that so many times I've wanted to fight fire with fire and ruin his reputation. A few weeks ago I almost justified it because I would be speaking the truth. But I know it's wrong, God. And I know how little you care about me seeking the approval of others. It pains me that he's a leader in The Edge. It probably pains you more. But because you loved me first; loved me before I cared about you; loved me when I could only think about myself; I forgive him. And I release the grudge I've been holding and the pain I feel. By the Blood of the Cross, Bless Andrew. Give him the love he needs. The love we all need."

I thought this was the end of his prayer. But he kept going,

"And forgive me for harboring such hatred toward him. I'm so sorry, Jesus. I can't see my blind spots and I know it. Who knows? Maybe I'm frustrated because I'm not serving anywhere and he's at least doing something. So prayers for Andrew and for me. I lift up both of us to you. Please give me the boldness to reconcile with him. Thank you, Jesus."

If only he could have heard our cheers!

After Kenya, Davis is attuned to the Counselor's voice. And he's hungry.

L

April 3

Littleton,

Great news!

Exciting work! To see Davis want to reconcile with Andrew shows a tremendous amount of spiritual growth. He's really starting to shine now. I just have a couple of additional thoughts.

Between Andrew's jealousy and Mark's isolation, Davis has had to struggle daily against discouragement and frustration. Although he probably wouldn't see it this way, these circumstances have all been God-ordained, and they have certainly grown his character. And now that Davis has repented of his attitude toward Andrew, try to work out an opportunity for the reconciliation he desires. Get the two of them alone quickly before the enemy can convince him it's not really necessary.

We had an angel on a similar type of mission ten years ago. His assignment was a young woman a few years after college. All the social tensions and the isolation, and the frustrations with roommates and neighbors and those closest to her, were strikingly similar to what Davis has been experiencing. In that case it turned out that the Lord used those tensions to help prepare her to meet her future husband. Her preparation was the same sort of heart surgery I see happening in young Davis. I know he's not even twenty but the parallels are strikingly similar. God may be using this time for the dual purpose of growing him closer to Jesus and preparing him for an eventual marriage.

So, as you go about campus making connections for him, send details about the young ladies in his social circles. Davis needs godly females who can show him a whole other side of the Lord that he can't learn from his male friends.

AM

April 4

Archangel Michael,

There's an interesting and clever young lady on campus who has come to my attention and might be perfect for Davis to meet. I've learned from one of the other angels her name is Ashley. Would you find out more?

Thanks,

L

April 5

Littleton,

Here's the dossier.

Name: Ashley Grace Sumner

Relationship to Davis: Both Freshmen on campus who have not yet met, although through Hampton and Caroline their social circles are getting closer.

Spiritual Biography: Ashley is from Birmingham, Alabama. She loves family and friends, and she sings on the worship team for TRU, the same thriving student ministry group Hampton and Caroline are involved in. The Holy Spirit gave her the spiritual gift of encouragement. Probably half of her text messages are uplifting notes to her friends. Someday she wants to walk down the aisle with Mr. Right. Apparently he needs to be handsome, clever, down to earth, cultured, and someone who loves the Lord–but he can't be, as she puts it, "too churchy." And because of her love of worship she hopes he will be a musician.

In Ashley's senior year of high school she went to prom with Ryan Nichols Brackleton, a friend from her church youth group. The two decided to date long distance when they went off to different colleges. Then the friction began.

Ashley has shared with her close friends that lately their dating relationship has changed and that she feels confused.

When Ashley visits his campus he doesn't really have anything planned. The last time she went he kept playing video games with his roommates while she sat there, occasionally being asked to play. Ashley doesn't like video games so it appears that he doesn't care much about her or her interests.

He goes to church every Sunday and is loosely involved with a student ministry. He still has a sweet side, but it seems he's become cynical about certain things: college life, the church, America in general to name just a few. The last time she visited he said that drugs can be harmful but he thinks recreational drugs should be legal. Ashley sat with his friends and listened to them, laughing and trying to engage with them, but she doesn't enjoy his crowd or think their jokes are funny.

Where was the guy she used to know? The clever one who loved the Lord and always tried to bring joy to people through his music? She needs to stay loyal to her high school sweetheart, right?

Ashley is in a Bible study led by none other than Caroline. Yes, Hampton's Caroline! One of our angels popped into her mind the idea that she should ask Caroline to stay late on Thursday to talk about her struggles.

Please follow-up right away with Caroline's response.

AM

April 5

Archangel Michael,

Caroline did well. Here's a transcript of part of the conversation she had with Ashley.

"I will be praying for you!" Caroline said. "You're asking some great questions and I want to encourage you in the Lord to keep seeking His guidance. As for guys, I can only say that you want to end up with someone who really loves Jesus. And he needs to be someone who prioritizes time with you, too. When do you and your boyfriend mostly talk?"

Ashley shrugged. "Mostly we just text late at night. I've visited him twice this year but he's yet to come here."

"And what do you guys talk about?"

"School and friends and how things are going. Now that I think about it, he does really talk more about what's going on with him and his friends."

"Hmm. And how about his friends? Do you like them?"

"I actually don't really care for his friends that much. They're okay, but they can be a little too sarcastic for me."

"Does being with him encourage you to grow closer to Jesus?"

"Well . . . not really, no. I pray a lot about our relationship so I'm closer to God that way. But we don't talk about God all that much."

"Well, do you think he has the character of someone you would want to marry?"

"I think he . . . did when we were in high school. That's a really good question, actually. Not right now, no."

"If the answer to both of those questions is no, then I'd break up with him," Caroline said, and then she reached out and touched Ashley's knee. "God is everything, Ashley! Listen, one of the most important things you can do is stay with a close group of girls who will help you to stay focused on the Lord. And remember, God can bring a true gentleman around. They are rare these days, and you'll want to be spiritually ready when he comes into your circles. If you want to be prepared for a relationship and marriage, you should work on your relationship with Jesus first. But don't grow close to Him for the purpose of hoping to meet someone. Do it because He loves you."

Great counsel. We need to produce more "Carolines" on this campus.

L

April 6

Archangel Michael,

Hampton invited Davis to his apartment so the two of them could talk about the presidential campaign. Hampton grilled a couple of steaks and cleared the living room table for them to go to work. Here's a brief but important excerpt from their conversation.

"I originally thought about your helping to get the word out to first-year students. It would pretty much have involved approaching as many people as possible and inviting them to vote. You have to be extroverted and shameless about talking to people you don't know. But having learned more about your background in history, and how much you enjoy American presidential biographies, I've changed my mind. I think you might do well in a VP position. This would mean helping me craft position papers, a campaign slogan, speech writing, etc. What do you think?"

"That sounds great! I love all of that stuff."

"You'll also need to be my partner in a two-person student debate in front of the whole campus. Are you comfortable with that?"

"Yeah, I'm comfortable."

"Great."

"But I want to be active in getting out the freshmen vote as well. At least in part. I have personal reasons."

"Personal reasons, huh? Anything you can share?"

"Well . . ." Davis scratched his chin and averted his eyes. "Honestly, getting rejected would do me some good. I still can't believe I was stupid enough to let myself drift so far from God. I just . . . "

"Hey!" Hampton put his hand on Davis's arm. "Everyone has drifted away from God at some point. Don't beat yourself up over it! It's not where you are now. Just remember, it's not flesh and blood we battle against. Spiritual war rages all around us. You've been too isolated, brother! Swimming upstream outside of a faith community, if you will. But Jesus has provided one for you now." Hampton clapped him on the shoulder. "The war . . . it's already been won at the Cross. Take the blessing and forget the past. It's over."

"Yeah, you're right. Thanks for the reminder." Davis grinned. "But I still want to be a part of getting out the vote."

"No problem. If you want to do both, you can do both. Just don't let it affect your grades."

The two then sat at the table with pencil and paper in hand and brainstormed on a variety of initiatives, including campaign speech tactics. They discussed student life on campus and the direction in which Hampton wanted to guide the university. And they discussed Hampton's philosophy of leadership at great length.

L

April 7

Archangel Michael,

Davis and Hampton had lunch at a local cafe. I think they're both realizing they could be good friends moving forward.

Hampton excused himself from the table for a bathroom break, and once out of Davis's sight he called Caroline and briefly told her about Davis. He asked her if she would be interested in allowing Davis to join in their dinner plans. Caroline said, "Sure . . . I can't wait to meet him!"

Hampton then returned to the table and said, "My girlfriend, Caroline, and I are having dinner tonight and we'd like you to join us if you don't have plans."

"Are you sure?"

"Absolutely. She's excited to meet you!"

"Great, I look forward to it."

"We'll pick you up at seven," Hampton said.

In the evening, Hampton picked up Caroline and Davis without telling them where they were going to eat. Apparently he does this often with Caroline . . . he likes to surprise her. Fifteen minutes later they pulled into the valet stand of one of the historic hotels in the area. The three of them had a two-and-a-half-hour dinner with lots of laughter and genuine conversation. There's a real sense of friendship forming in a way that only the Lord can bring about. Davis watched with hawklike intensity the way Hampton and Caroline interacted. I think he found it much in line with what Robert expressed during the last haircut. At least, I hope that was the case!

After they dropped Davis off for the night, Hampton told Caroline, "Good kid, isn't he? I've invited him to come to TRU and have been thinking about places to plug him in."

Caroline brightened and clapped her hands together. "Please do!" she said. "He's . . ." She sighed and smiled.

"What? What is it?" Hampton asked.

"Well, he's kind of a gentleman. And I was just talking with a friend of mine about how God could bring a gentleman into her life. She's fresh out of a bad relationship, but maybe, just maybe . . ."

Hampton laughed. "Okay, I see where you're going with this. But remember—I need his head in the game for the campaign."

"I'm hoping to introduce them, not arrange their marriage." Caroline wrinkled her nose at Hampton and poked his shoulder. "Don't go putting the cart before the horse!"

After that, their conversation turned to other things, but I like the direction of their thoughts when it comes to Davis and Ashley! It's all very encouraging!

L

April 8

Archangel Michael,

Here's a recap of Davis's first night at TRU.

Davis received a lot of attention after walking in with Hampton and Caroline. Several students approached him right away, welcoming him and asking questions. Davis was kind to everybody and consciously tried to remember the names of the new people he met. As the music started and people took their seats, a special-needs student started shouting out, "Church time! Church time! Everyone sit down!"

It quickly became clear that his behavior caused a few people to feel awkward. A couple of heads turned, and one or two people smiled, but the people nearby didn't seem to know how to respond. Davis closed his eyes for a moment and whispered something the preacher in Africa had said, "America needs to use its power for the Lord. Any influence is power."

Then he opened his eyes, excused himself from Hampton and Caroline, and sat down in the chair right next to this student. He introduced himself as Caroline looked on. She turned and raised her eyebrows at Ashley, who was watching from across the room. Ashley inconspicuously pointed at Davis and mouthed, "Wow." Caroline grinned.

After the service we navigated conversations so Davis would mix with a particular group of guys Jesus wanted him to meet. I had Davis walk up to them as a student from Alabama . . . clearly one of the best storytellers in the group . . . was recapping the weekend to his friends. He had gone home to participate in his older brother's wedding.

"They bought all of us groomsmen a barber-chair shave from a traditional, licensed barber. And I'll tell you what—I decided that from now on I would only shave with a straight blade razor. And I will *only* get my haircut in a traditional barbershop. No plastic razors. No salons. And the other guys were totally with me. All of us—and I mean *all* of us–purchased straight blade razors with safety guards, and bought a kit that included a coffee mug with a brush and that special soap barbers use."

Davis really enjoyed this story. I can tell by how he grinned and nodded along that he felt at home and easy with them.

I also received a special message about a guy in this group named Nathan, who is from Baltimore. The Lord wanted Davis to meet him right away. It wasn't hard to do! After the wedding story, Nathan introduced himself to Davis, and after finding out that Davis knew how to row, he invited him to cover an open seat in a regatta this weekend. Nathan is part of the glue that holds TRU together, and with the shared experience of rowing between them I think he and Davis could turn out to be fast friends.

Davis also met a guy from Alexandria, Virginia, who was comically vulnerable when talking about his dating situation. "Guys, I'm sunk! The year is ruined! The girl I took to the dance on Saturday is avoiding me. She hasn't respond to my texts. Ahhhh! We were so perfect together! Check out this picture of us. See, we're perfect together!"

This same group of guys mentioned that they had plans to pick up some of the girls, including Ashley, on Saturday night before heading to a bluegrass festival in the neighboring town. They invited Davis and he accepted. Nathan mentioned that he had cigars waiting for them at his condo after they dropped off the girls.

When Davis returned to his empty dorm room he fell on his knees praising God as the Giver of all good things.

I'll fill you in on the bluegrass festival in the next letter.

L

April 9

Archangel Michael,

It's amazing how much a spiritual reservoir can fill up during a bluegrass music festival, followed by late night cigars!

The group piled into a large SUV and drove by open fields, listening to familiar songs on their way to the festival. Davis loved the fellowship, and I watched Ashley listen closely to everything he said. She seemed to be taking note of how important the Lord is in his life, and she managed to slip in a question or two about his background. At this point I'm unsure if this means anything significant, but we can most certainly say it is *not nothing*.

Davis laughed a lot and was easygoing, especially with Nathan. He initially seemed pretty blind to the girls in the car, but that changed later. Eventually conversations switched to how the Lord might be at work on their campus. This conversation spanned across student groups, social environments, ministry movements, roommates, academics, dating, student leadership, and the arts. It was during this time that I saw Davis notice Ashley for the first time. He watched her with rapt attention while she was talking, and when nobody was paying attention to him I heard him whisper under his breath, "She's sweet and . . . sharp." And then he added in prayer, "Lord, she's *really beautiful*."

By the way, the bluegrass festival was an ideal way for Davis to fellowship with his new friends. It was a carefree outdoor environment where they could talk and laugh rather openly. Dancing started later in the evening. Ashley watched Davis dance with everyone, purposefully asking girls who hadn't yet been asked. Lots of pictures were taken and shared, and random conversations about the night's events continued on the way home.

The gentlemen dropped off the ladies and then went to Nathan's place to smoke cigars. This made for some great male bonding. Davis seemed impressed by Nathan's vintage Regatta posters, his set of vinyl albums, and the humidor his grandfather had purchased for him. They stayed up talking and laughing until three o'clock in the morning.

L

April 10

Littleton,

Well done. I'm excited for Davis. Now that he's finally connected to a Christian community, he'll invite Jesus into more and more of his life, and our enemies will have less and less influence on him. We're going to have a field day on the battlefield.

I look forward to hearing more.

AM

April 11

Archangel Michael,

University Auditorium: The Student Debate

Hampton and Davis sat at a table with a microphone in front of a fairly representative portion of the student body. Ashley, Caroline, Nathan, and several others from the student ministry sat in the front row of the audience, along with Cody. Andrew arrived with some of his friends from The Edge, and they sat toward the back. Even Mark, Davis's roommate, came, sitting in the back by himself. And Elizabeth came, too. She and Davis haven't spoken much since he decided on the Kenya trip at the last minute instead of going to the Bahamas.

Opening remarks by a university dean were followed by the two presidential candidates facing off in a challenging debate. Hampton did extremely well against a formidable opponent. The two finished with Hampton as a clear frontrunner. Then it was time for the two vice-presidential candidates to debate. Davis faced an upperclassman, a junior with student government experience.

The Speaker: "For the last part of our debate, we will now turn to the Vice Presidents. Gentlemen, please tell us what leadership in student affairs means to you. I'm hoping for a short exchange that might high-light any differences in your platform. Carlton, we'll begin with you."

"Carlton: I think about last year, how Craig and I led the Student Affairs committee and brought in Senator Chase to be a guest speaker for our campus. We didn't have a lot of time and budgets were tight, but the student body needed something like that. So we lobbied for it and then we got it. The night was a great success. And everyone was shocked to hear that we pulled it off."

The Speaker: "Thank you, Carlton. Your time is up. Davis, do you have a reply?"

Carlton: "Mr. Speaker, I don't mean to interrupt, but Davis was in high school last year. So he might need to talk about high school. Just wanted you to know that's fine by me."

Reading between the lines, I'm guessing this comment was meant to undercut Davis. Caroline and Ashley were quiet and seemed tense. Hampton had his hands clasped in prayer under the table. Andrew looked straight ahead and rubbed his chin. Carlton then sat down and smirked. The rest of the debate should have been a breeze for him. Davis wouldn't have much to say.

But he was wrong. Davis looked out into the crowd and met Ashley's gaze. There was a slight pause. Then he began.

"Mr. Speaker, I'd like to continue with Carlton's example if that's okay. Carlton, if I could ask, when did y'all first decide to bring in Senator Chase?"

"Late January," Carlton said, rising to his feet.

"And how did you decided to allocate the money for a guest speaker?"

"I'd heard him speak before, and he's really good. And tough. Knows what he's talking about. Students could use that sort of influence."

"I see. Thank you. And the event happened in late April?"

"Yeah, it did. Why?"

"I just wanted to know how it all went down. I actually did face a similar environment last year at my school. We had a budget to spend and a few months to do it. But we took a different approach."

"Oh . . . how so?"

"We sent a survey out to the student body asking for their input. Then we made our decisions after reading their suggestions."

Carlton responded quickly, "We didn't have time. I had to book our Senator."

"You had three months. And it only takes a few hours, maybe a day at most, to get feedback online."

"He's a busy man, and he's the best around. Wouldn't you agree? Or don't you know much about our State's leadership?

"Oh, I know him quite well. But that's not the point. You're changing the subject. We're talking about leadership in student affairs. And you just sort of did what you wanted."

"Look, you've gotta do your best and have the courage to wield your power when opportunity knocks. I'd do it again."

"You mentioned that 'leadership is being your best and having the courage to wield power.' Did I quote you correctly?"

"Yes."

"I assume this is a core part of your leadership position?

"Yes, it is. As I already said."

Titters of laughter in the audience. Davis waited until they quieted to continue.

"If that's true, then you must be saying students should choose the strongest people to lead them, and then get out of their way?"

"I'd prefer to say, 'trust their instincts' rather than 'get out of their way.' But in so many words, yes. You can get more done that way."

"It seems to me your whole outlook on the student body is the survival of the fittest. It reminds me of what the philosopher Nietzsche said about asserting your will on the world. There are those who do it, and those who don't because they are too weak. Egoism is noble."

"Look, I think we're not naïve about things. Life's tough, and people want leaders who not only get that but who can get things done in the midst of it."

"I disagree. I think we're exposing a real difference between our teams. Leadership isn't domination; leadership is service."

"That *sounds* nice . . . but what does that *mean*? Why don't you tell us how you came up with that idea?

"I didn't come up with that idea. It's been said before."

"By who?"

"Since you asked, it would be Jesus."

"Ohhhh, I see. So you're playing the religious card. Trying to get votes." He rolled his eyes for the audience and continued. "Tell everyone this, how does your platform follow Jesus?"

"Jesus said the greatest of those among you are those who serve. And service is caring for another . . . getting to know your people really well. Being with them and looking out for their best interests."

"Don't you think it's kind of risky for our student body to vote for a team who . . . all of a sudden decides that *being nice* is the best way to govern?"

"I didn't say being nice is our method for governing. I said aiming to serve others with mutual respect, I might add, is a stronger foundation than saying, 'We are strong; follow us.'"

"Look, we get results. And that's what students really want. You're asking people to vote for some noble way of doing things, but you have no weight behind what you say. If you were really honest you might as well say, 'vote for us, we have some new ideas about leadership that sound really nice.'"

Several people in the audience laughed.

Davis waited for the laughter to die down, and then he continued in a calm voice. "Not exactly. Our ideas aren't new. I never said that. Actually," he smiled, "I said just the opposite. Jesus lived a long time ago."

"Wait, wait, wait." His opponent waved his arm in the air. "Now that's not really fair, because nobody can really be like *Jesus*."

"No, but they can become more like him and follow his way of leading. I actually know a guy who did this. Great leader, everyone loved him. They didn't fear him."

"Oh, here you go again. With more smiley, happy pictures of leadership. Who is this guy? A friend of yours from high school? Tell us. What's his name?"

"George Washington."

Whoops and hollers arose from the audience, and from more than just Davis and Hampton's established supporters. Ashley and Caroline were amongst the loudest. Andrew actually applauded, too. So did Mark. Davis stepped back with a smile on his face—not a smirk of prideful superiority but a smile of confident victory—and crossed his arms, waiting for his opponent to give a response. Carlton stood with his mouth open and his eyes blinking, the horrified expression of defeat suddenly realized too late, plastered on his face. He sputtered to make a response when the room quieted down, but he couldn't seem to formulate his thoughts. With a sigh and a shake of his head, he conceded the floor back to Davis.

The Speaker: "Davis, do you have any final remarks?"

"Just one thing." Davis then looked out into the crowd and said, "Students . . . Vote for Hampton. Because it is *your* school."

And the VP debate ended earlier than he anticipated. Davis thanked his opponent for participating in the debate and shook his hand, clearly wanting no enmity between them. I observed Carlton actually smiling while he shook Davis's hand.

"Brilliant, man," his opponent said. "I can't even be mad about that. Best debate I've ever been a part of. You sure you're not a little like Nietzsche at heart?"

"Quite sure," Davis said.

Ashley smiled as she watched the exchange from the audience. After the debate, lots of students rushed up to congratulate Davis. But to his surprise—and mine also—Andrew was the first one in line.

"Great job, Davis! I'm so proud of you for mentioning Jesus!" Andrew said.

"Andrew! I really appreciate your coming. Hey, I'm sorry I've harbored bad feelings about you this year. I know that's kept us distant. Will you forgive me?"

"Absolutely! But please forgive me, too, for the same."

"Of course. Look forward to catching up with you later tonight!" said Davis.

Elizabeth was next in line, and she stood with her arms crossed over her chest, not reaching out for Davis to shake his hand or to give him a hug. "Hey," she said. "That was great. Really great."

"Thanks," Davis said. "Hey, uh, I know we've hardly talked since spring break, but . . . "

"It's okay. I just wanted to let you know I'm seeing someone now, and it's serious, and I don't want there to be any hard feelings between us."

"Right! Of course not," Davis said.

"Good." Elizabeth smiled. "Well, that's it, I guess. I hope you win the election. You've got my vote!"

"Thank you. See you around."

Davis and Hampton stayed until the room closed down, receiving every student who wanted to visit with them afterwards. Ashley opened the Bible app on her phone and flipped through the verses she had saved. She stopped and read Psalm 45:2:

"You are the most handsome of the sons of men;
grace is poured upon your lips;
therefore God has blessed you forever."

I watched all of this with great joy. Davis was perfectly in step with his calling and giftedness.

L

April 12

Archangel Michael,

Post-Debate follow-up the next day:

Davis and Hampton went to a seafood restaurant in town. They talked about the campaign for a while, and then they had this little exchange.

"Thanks so much for plugging me into TRU and inviting me into your campaign. I had a blast last night, but beyond that, I finally feel like I'm getting on the right track. I really appreciate it."

"Sure man, my pleasure. I'm so glad we got reconnected."

Davis then excused himself for the bathroom. A minute later, Hampton's phone vibrated. It was a text message from Caroline.

The text read:

"Ashley's coming over right now. She said she's ready to start dating again, and that she really loved seeing Davis in the debate! Do y'all want to join us? :)"

Hampton smiled and put his phone down, and Davis returned to his chair.

Hampton looked up and said, "Caroline just mentioned Ashley is coming over to her place. Your name came up in a . . . *positive way*, if you know what I mean." He grinned and raised his eyebrows. "She asked me if we want to join them."

Just then, the waitress interrupted and said, "The food will be out shortly, gentlemen."

Davis leaned in and said to the waitress, "Check please, right away." He then quickly scanned the room and said, "Give the meals to that elderly couple in the corner," and he offered his credit card.

"Okay . . . ," the waitress said, hesitant. "Are you sure?"

"I've got to go meet a girl," Davis said.

"Oh, I see!" The waitress laughed. "I'll be right back."

"Quick, please!" Davis called after her.

She raised a hand in acknowledgment. Davis bounced his knee until the waitress returned with his credit card and a small to-go container. "If you're going to see a girl, you should always bring chocolate," she said with a broad smile. "On the house, Sweetie."

Davis peeked into the container to find two chocolate éclairs. "Great idea. Thanks!"

"No problem. Go get her. And keep an eye on him," she said to Hampton. "He's a little too lovesick for his own good."

"Oh, I will," Hampton said. "Come on, lover boy. I guess real food can wait."

L

April 13

Littleton,

These stories stir my heart and fill me with confidence about Davis's future. Your service to Davis has been truly excellent, and now it's drawing to an end.

I found out this morning that I'm being reassigned to a different college campus. Don't worry, I see the spiritual trajectory Davis is on and can anticipate how the year will end for him. He's on fire for Jesus, plugged into a solid Christian community, and reconciled with a brother in Christ with whom he'd had a year of conflict. You've fought a lot of battles to help him find his place, and you've introduced him to an exceptional young lady whom he is ready to pursue. He's an exciting young man who can do a lot for the kingdom.

Our correspondence will now be shared with every angel on the campaign team. I'm sure it will be invaluable. Given that university life is one of our targeted campaigns, and judging from the resources we're allotted and the ground we're gaining, we're anticipating a spiritual breakthrough across college campuses, one heart at a time.

It has truly been a joy serving with you, Littleton. I'm signing off now, and you have been specially requested to sing in the Heavenly Choir before your next assignment begins. I expect you'll want to linger for a day or two to say goodbye to Davis, but do not linger too long. Everyone can't wait to see you on Sunday morning at 11:00 hours. We shall Worship the King!

Glory to God.
Glory to God, in the Highest.
And Peace, on Earth.
Good Will toward Men.

AM

GROUP DISCUSSION QUESTIONS

- What is the primary spiritual difference between Ashley and Elizabeth?

- What is the most important thing that happened to Davis his first year? What about the second most important?

- What is Davis's chief struggle? Is it unique to him, common to everyone, or a combination of the two?

- When you think of "warfare" do you get scared or excited? What would Jesus say?

- Discuss the book's portrayal of a spiritual war waging between heaven and earth. What do you think about it?

- How, specifically, do Jonathan, Jason, Robert, Cody, and Hampton encourage Davis's walk with Christ. How are they different?

- What do you learn about leadership from Archangel Michael's letters? How about Littleton's?

- Describe Caroline's influence on Ashley. What does she do well?

- What advice would you give Cody? Elizabeth? Andrew? Davis?

- Has this book made you think more about how spiritual warfare influences your own life?

About the Author...

Nicholas Cappas has Master's Degrees in English from Wake Forest University and the University of Birmingham (England) & in Divinity from Baylor University. He lives in Atlanta, Georgia, working as a freelance copywriter and serving in student ministry.

56747444R00107

Made in the USA
Charleston, SC
30 May 2016